LOOSE ENDS

Dorothy Stewart

This edition published 2024 worldwide by Loaves & Fishes

Copyright © 2024 Dorothy Stewart

The right of Dorothy Stewart to be identified as the author of this work has been asserted in accordance with the Copyright, Designs & Patents Act 1988.

All rights reserved. No part of this publication may be reproduced, stored in a retrieval system, or transmitted in any form or by any means, electronic, mechanical, photocopying or otherwise, without the prior written permission of the publisher.

Scripture quotations are taken from the Holy Bible, New International Version® NIV®. Copyright ©1973, 1978, 1984, 2011 by Biblica, Inc. Used with permission. All rights reserved worldwide.

This is a work of fiction. Names, characters, places and incidents are either the product of the author's imagination or used fictitiously. Except where actual historical events and characters are being described for the storyline of this novel, all situations in this publication are fictitious and any resemblance to actual persons, living or dead, business establishments, events or locales is purely coincidental.

Cover design by Liz Carter

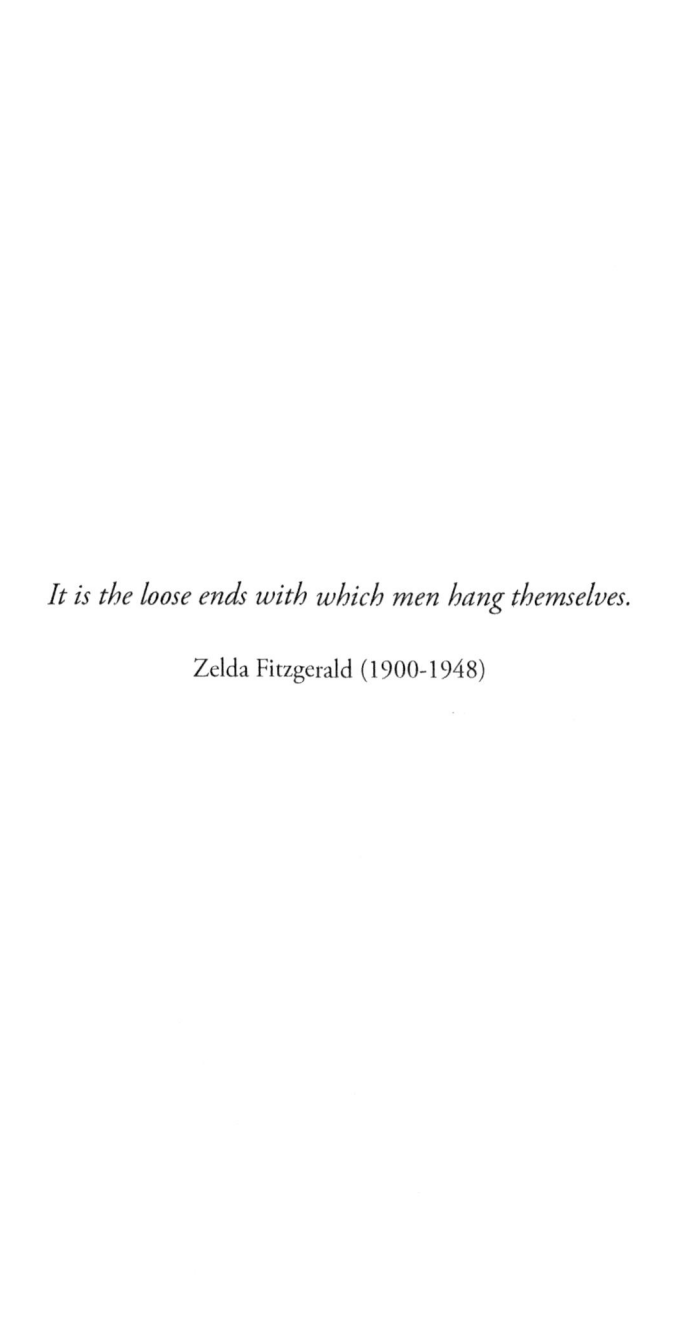

It is the loose ends with which men hang themselves.

Zelda Fitzgerald (1900-1948)

CHAPTER 1

❖

Jill stretched contentedly. It was a soft October morning and for a change she had time to sit and think. Her desk in the study faced the little orchard behind the house where mist was rising like white ghosts from the grass. She reached down to stroke Barney the muscular tabby cat who was weaving around her ankles, then she lifted her mug of coffee and sipped, enjoying the strong taste and the luxury of time to savour it.

Life seemed to plunge on without time to get everything done, let alone to stand and stare. She looked down at her notes for the church service she was due to lead later that morning. They were really rather scrappy. Thank goodness there was now time to work on them and produce something better. The congregation certainly deserved it. Jill set down her mug, picked up her pen and got down to work.

She felt a bit guilty to so relish this time alone. Poor Hugo was having to work yet another weekend away from home in Birmingham. The reorganisation after the dratted take-over seemed to be dragging on and on. Jill had not understood why a successful Somerset auction house should want to take over what seemed to be a pretty run-down Birmingham outfit, but no doubt there were good business reasons for it. Hugo, as Finance Director, could be relied on for working out the advantages to his firm, though latterly it seemed to be taking up and more of his time and energy.

He had not even had time to ring her – not since his late-night call on Friday. Nor had she had much time to talk to him during the week either. They were both so busy. The local primary school, where she was headmistress, was always hectic and this week had included a lengthy Parents Evening. She and Hugo had planned to have supper at their favourite restaurant afterwards but the Parents Evening had taken much more time than expected and they had just come home and crashed. He had left for Birmingham first thing the next morning.

Jill sighed. Maybe there would be time to catch up when he got home later today. She bent to her notes and was soon absorbed.

A sudden loud knocking on the back door broke through her concentration. Startled, she rose from her desk. It would be one of the neighbours from the lane that ran alongside the house. Some of the farmer's cows had probably got loose again, or could it be the pigs this time? They were masters of escapology and turned up to rootle around the little orchard behind the house every year once the apples started falling.

With a smile, she walked though to the kitchen and opened the back door. A very young policeman stood on the doorstep, turning his uniform cap round and round in his hands.

'Hello,' Jill said. 'What can I do for you?'

'Mrs Leiston?' He swallowed hard and stumbled on the name.

'Yes?'

'Can I come in?'

'Is something the matter?' she asked. Why would a policeman turn up on her doorstep and want to come in, she wondered. Then she remembered: when her father died, a policewoman had turned up to tell her mother… her elderly mother, now frail with that horrid emphysema.

'Is it my mother?' Jill asked quickly. 'Has something happened?'

'Please,' the young policeman repeated. 'Can I come in?'

'Look, you can just tell me,' Jill assured him.

'Please!' The young policeman seemed agonised with embarrassment. 'Please, let me come in and then I'll tell you.'

Jill shrugged. 'Oh, all right then. Come through this way', and she led him through the kitchen to the study. Looking closely at him, she saw how pale he was.

'Would you like to sit down?' she asked.

He shook his head and she could see the effort he was making to stand straight and appear official and in charge.

'I think, madam, that *you* should sit down,' he said.

'Why?' Jill asked. 'I'm fine and nothing you're going to tell me is going to be a shock. My mother's elderly and…'

The young man broke in, 'It's not your mother.' He stopped and took a deep breath before plunging on. 'The thing is… I've come to tell you… It's your husband…'

'Hugo?'

The name came out sharply. For a moment, time itself seemed to stop. She forced herself to ask sensible questions.

'Has he had an accident? Is that it? Is he all right?'

How she hated those motorways and the heavy traffic. Hugo had never enjoyed driving even though she thought he was perfectly competent and safe. Still, she always worried when he was away from home on a business trip.

The young policeman's words came out in a rush as he unburdened himself of his message.

'I'm sorry, Mrs Leiston, your husband has been found dead. It looks like he's committed suicide, I'm afraid. Overdose.'

Done, the boy took a deep breath and waited, his eyes fixed on her face. Jill stared at him. Hugo dead? She fought down the rising tide of shock.

'No,' she said, shaking her head. 'No, I'm sure that can't be right. It must be someone else. My husband is in Birmingham on business. I spoke to him on Friday evening. He said things were going all right and he would be home today, in time for lunch.' The echo of his voice was fresh in Jill's mind. 'So you see, it must be someone else. Mistaken identity.'

'I'm sorry,' the policeman insisted. 'I'm afraid it *is* your husband. The local police were called out by a dog walker… He was found in the fort on Brean Down.'

A sudden vivid picture of the old fort flashed into Jill's mind. Grey stone walls and a maze of empty buildings and gun emplacements filling the very tip of the almost-island jutting out into the Bristol Channel. Brean Down was one of their favourite places. The climb up to the top was a bit daunting but the views of the Bristol Channel and the lovely walks down to the fort – not to mention the old fort itself – made it well worth it. They had been there for a walk only a few months ago…

The young man was still talking and Jill had to force herself to concentrate.

'They've taken ... his body ... to Weston General Hospital,' he was saying. 'Somebody will need to identify it. Is there anyone who could...?'

'Oh, I'll do that,' Jill said automatically. 'There's nobody else.'

Hugo was an only child, his parents long dead. Jill was the only close family he had. They had not had any children of their own. She realised her mind was wandering again and she wondered at her response. Did it mean that she had accepted 'the body' was Hugo's? How could it be? She shoved the rising panic down again. The police clearly were convinced. No doubt they had checked the identity of ... the body they had found. Hugo would have had credit cards, his diary, wallet, mobile phone with him...

She felt strangely distant from everything. It simply could not be true, yet there seemed to be so many facts. She tried the words over again to herself in her mind: 'Hugo. Dead.' Her mind was functioning but it was like operating from behind plate glass. Strange. She had to make an effort to pay attention.

The young policeman seemed relieved to be dealing with practical matters, and was now brisk and matter of fact, giving her the telephone number of the coroner's officer, the person she would have to talk to at the hospital mortuary. Jill wrote it all down and thanked him. She was aware he seemed surprised at how calm she was.

'Will you be all right?' he asked. 'Is there someone...?'

He seemed taken aback by her sudden burst of laughter. She squelched it, realising how unseemly it must have appeared.

'Yes, I'll be all right,' she told him. 'And there is certainly Someone to look after me. I'm a lay preacher and I've got a service to do at 10.30 this morning. I'm sure God won't take the day off just when I need Him.'

The young man looked confused. 'I meant…'

'I know,' she told him gently. 'You meant people. Visible people with skin on. Please don't worry. I've got plenty of friends…'

'Well, I'll be going then.' He looked relieved and suddenly itching to be gone.

Jill led him back through the kitchen to the back door. As he stood awkwardly on the step, she said, 'Thank you for coming. I know it wasn't easy for you. First time you've had to do something like this, was it?'

A grin flitted briefly across his face until he recalled the circumstances and he managed another solemn look. 'I'm very sorry…'

'Yes,' she told him. 'I know. Off you go now and get yourself a cup of tea!'

CHAPTER 2

✤

It was a relief to close the door. Going back through the kitchen to her desk in the study was like sleepwalking. The day was still beautiful with the mist still lifting in fine veils from the grass. She ran the words again in her head: 'Hugo is dead.' It could not be true. How could he be dead? Yet the police were sure.

She reached for the telephone and called her friend, Eleanor. She was the minister of the group of churches Jill helped out with lay preaching.

After telling her the news and accepting her sympathy, Jill asked, 'Should I carry on with the service? I feel perfectly fine. It's not real to me yet. What do you think?'

'If you can do it, I think it will do you good,' Eleanor told her. 'It will give you a couple of hours' breathing space, focusing on something else, not having to think about it. Then when you come up for air, you'll be able to think more clearly about it and what you have to do.'

'I'll do it then,' Jill decided firmly. But first things first. Another phone call, this time to the coroner's officer at the mortuary to make arrangements to view and identify the body. *The body.* It just was not real. Hugo was a strong, fit man, full of life, a vibrant physical presence. She could not think of him as 'the body'. A dead body. What would it look like? The idea threatened to overturn her precarious calm. She put the thought away and went to get ready.

Church was fine, full of friends and familiar faces. Jill took a few moments after the service to tell her closest friend, Monica Harris, what had happened.

'You'll come to us for lunch,' Monica told her firmly. 'No use going home to your place.'

And Jill realised she had not thought ahead at all, beyond getting through the service and then somehow getting to the mortuary. Life did not seem smooth and logical any longer.

Monica and her husband, Geoffrey, hovered over her all the way through lunch, behaving as if she were ill. Jill was startled to realise she found that funny. She simply did not feel she needed this extra attention. There was nothing wrong with *her*.

After lunch, Monica and Geoffrey announced that they would drive her over to Weston-super-Mare to the hospital where the mortuary was and then bring her back home to Somerton afterwards.

'It's not something you should do on your own,' they said.

But she still had to walk into that anteroom on her own and wait, in a kind of limbo, for the curtain to be drawn back and the shape on the stainless-steel trolley revealed.

The attendant pulled back the sheet to reveal Hugo's face. His hair was a bright aureole like a fluffy halo. Most men his age were thinning or going bald, but Hugo still had a thick thatch of beautiful white hair which he always kept immaculate. His eyes were slightly open as though he were looking at her sideways.

The man asked her if she recognised the body.

'Yes,' she said, her voice coming out muffled and low. 'That's my husband, Hugo.'

And so it was true. Hugo was dead. He would never be coming home again, large and noisy and filling the house with his presence.

The attendant drew the sheet back over Hugo's face, pulled the curtains closed, and left Jill to sit on the overstuffed banquette in the anteroom to collect herself.

Something was wrong but she could not make her brain think what it was. Then she thought: 'This is silly. Yes, I've done what *they* wanted. I've identified the body for them. But I haven't done what *I* want, what *I* need to do – and that is to say goodbye to Hugo…' So she rose and went out and found an attendant and asked, and once again the curtains were drawn back and the sheet pulled down.

And then she had time to look, really look. And it really was her beloved Hugo, and he was so very completely dead. Not looking as though he were asleep. Asleep he looked like a little boy, always with a smile curving his lips. Dead, he looked blank and almost angry, with those blue eyes just visible between his eyelids.

She tangled her fingers in his hair, a last caress, and leaned over to kiss him goodbye.

When she said she was ready, the attendant gently ushered her through for the next stage in the process. Another room with those uncomfortable banquettes and institutional chairs, and Monica, steadfast friend, and the coroner's officer waiting for her.

First he took a statement, questioning her about Hugo's state of mind in the previous weeks, and whether they had had any problems.

'Well, he was very busy with things at work,' she told him. 'More than usual, yes. There was all that Millennium Bug nonsense at the beginning of the year. Then, after the take-over and all the documents they had to produce, there seemed to be more work than ever. He was Finance Director, at Russett & Thomson, the art and antiques auction house in Ilminster.'

Another question.

'Yes, it took him away from home much more than in the past. Lots more meetings, that sort of thing. He had to go up to Birmingham for quite a lot of them. That's where the firm they took over – Aston Antique Sales – was based.'

Jill suddenly realised how vague she was being, in fact how vague she was about it all. Maybe she had not paid enough attention, shown enough interest in what Hugo was doing, what was going on in his life. She sent a silent heartfelt message to him: 'If I wasn't paying enough attention, I'm sorry. If I didn't support you when you needed me…'

Another question from the coroner's officer broke into her thoughts. She tried to focus.

'Yes, he spent a lot of extra time at work recently. Yes, evenings and weekends.'

And finally the questions were over. She had to sign a few things: her statement – transformed into official police-speak which her teacher's mind noticed was barely recognisable as what she had said – and a receipt. A large transparent polythene sack was handed over to her and she saw it contained Hugo's jacket, his wallet, and a jumble of other things. For a moment, she stared at it in horror. She could not bear to touch it.

Monica put her hand reassuringly on Jill's arm. 'Come on, you can look at those things later. Let's get you home.'

It was the same long vinyl-floored hospital corridor that she had walked down but now the sleepwalking had a different feeling. It was not sleep. It had become a waking, walking nightmare. Because that *was* Hugo dead on that cold stainless-steel trolley. And she was going away and leaving him there. It was not like when he had been in hospital before and she knew she would see him again and he would be coming home soon, fit and well. This time it was all wrong. She was walking away and he was being left behind. And she was carrying his things in this ugly plastic bag.

Zombie-like she followed her friends out to their car and sat, in shock and silence, as they drove her back to their house where she had left her car. She pulled herself together enough to drive home, turning the car gratefully into the drive at the side of the house.

It was the same house that she had woken up to at seven o'clock that Sunday morning yet now it was different. Now it was empty and strange. She felt she did not belong here any more. She dropped the big plastic sack on the sitting room floor and wandered round the house, from room to room. She knew she should make something to eat but she felt no hunger. She felt nothing at all.

She had been so eager to be alone, away from trying to please her kind friends with appropriate responses to their caring enquiries till she could scream.

'Yes, I'll be fine. Honest. Yes, I'll ring you if I need anything. Yes, honestly. I'll be fine.'

The cat flap clattered and Barney the cat appeared, glaring accusingly at her. Jolted into action, she found a tin of cat food and ladled a decent amount into his bowl, then stood and watched as he scoffed it. At least she could do this…

She wandered back to the sitting room and stood looking at the ugly plastic sack she had brought back from the hospital. Finally getting together enough courage, she knelt down beside it and reached in to pull Hugo's jacket out of it. She could smell his pipe smoke on it. Idly she tried the jacket pockets. There was nothing in any of them. Clearly the police had searched, and the things Hugo usually carried stuffed into his jacket pockets were lying at the bottom of the sack. She tipped the contents out on to the floor. There was Hugo's wallet, empty of the money she had already signed the receipt for, but still containing his various membership cards and credit cards, and a yellowing newspaper cutting listing market days in all the local towns. She loved going to markets and Hugo always made sure that if there was a market anywhere on their day trips out she would not miss it.

She set out on the carpet beside her his tobacco pouch, pipe, matches, pocket-knife. Handkerchief. The usual mix of pens and pencils. His diary she noted was made out with appointments for the weeks ahead. The diary entries suggested a life that would continue into the foreseeable future. There was no sign that he had cancelled anything.

At the very bottom of the sack were two books, both brand-new. One was an action-packed novel of the kind Hugo loved. There was a bookmark tucked in neatly at page 30. The other was the latest crime novel by her favourite author. Hugo always brought her back a book she wanted as a little gift from his trips away. She held the book close to her heart and whispered a thank you. It was so sweet of him to remember.

Mechanically she took everything upstairs as if she were tidying up after him. Not that Hugo ever needed it. He was the tidiest of people. She hung his jacket in his wardrobe and placed his other things on his bedside table, setting the novel he had bought for her on hers.

Then she went downstairs and stared blankly at the television until it was time for bed. Finally came the routine of locking up, extra carefully after the little break-in they had had a few weeks ago. Neighbours reckoned there were travellers in the area just trying their luck. Well, they had not found anything to steal – or maybe Jill had disturbed them. Whichever it was, they had not had time to take anything as far as she had been able to see or do any real damage, except for the gouge marks round the lock on the back door.

And so at last to bed. Light out and time for her bedtime prayers. But what words did she have? The numbness seemed to have taken over her ability to speak to God. It was like one of those awful silences in the middle of a telephone conversation when you cannot think what to say but neither can you simply hang up.

Too weary to fight, Jill simply let the silence stretch. God would understand, she was sure. And then suddenly, as she turned towards the other pillow, with the faint scent of Hugo still lingering there, the enormity of it all hit her like a tidal wave. Blindly she seized the pillow and burrowed her face into it, taking enormous breaths of the familiar but fading scent. And into her mind came a picture of Hugo, dying alone, his back against the wall of the old fort.

'Oh, Hugo…!'

And her cry rose like the howl of an animal in pain, echoing out into the empty darkness.

CHAPTER 3

THE DAYS THAT followed seemed to blur into one another. At first, there were lots of kind phone calls, condolence cards and letters. The messages were thoughtful and supportive and Jill felt warmed and comforted by them. Friends dropped by with flowers as if she were ill, and she had to admit she did feel very strange. Life seemed so unreal.

The obvious things that needed doing – like arranging Hugo's funeral – had to be put on hold. Monica's husband Geoffrey, who was their solicitor as well as long-time friend, had explained that first there would have to be a post mortem and then an inquest. No one seemed to know how long it would take. For Jill it felt like limbo.

Someone came from Hugo's firm. Tall and well-dressed, in his early 50s, the man introduced himself as James Wheatley, Finance Director from the Birmingham end, who would now be taking over from Hugo as Group FD.

Jill thought it was kind of him to visit, until he explained, sitting relaxed in an armchair in her comfortable sitting room, a mug of tea balanced on his knee, 'We'd noticed a few discrepancies, you see. I'm afraid your husband had been – I'm sorry, there's no way to soften this – he'd been embezzling from the company and the take-over brought the discrepancies to light.'

Jill exclaimed in disbelief, but Wheatley continued smoothly, 'We had alerted him to the fact that we were aware of his activities, to give him time to put things right before he retired, but clearly he chose another option – one we couldn't have envisaged.'

It sounded like a prepared speech, rather like the young policeman who had come to tell her the news of Hugo's death. Maybe, Jill thought, that was the only way people could cope with having to break bad news.

'I'm terribly sorry. We're all terribly sorry.'

As the meaning of what Wheatley had said slowly trickled down into Jill's mind, she found herself staring at him, struggling to take it in. Hugo had been embezzling – from the firm that he had been instrumental in setting up? Hugo, who was the straightest, most honest person in the world? The man who became so indignant about any kind of deceit? She could not imagine the man she had known and loved and lived with for so long doing anything dishonest.

But James Wheatley was continuing to talk. 'You'll have noticed he was spending a lot of extra time at the office? He was attempting to cover his tracks…'

'I don't believe you!'

The words burst out, outrage making Jill's eyes bright and bringing sudden colour to her cheeks. She glared at the man, hating him and everything he was saying, but inside she began to tremble. She could not believe him, she did not want to believe him, yet this whole nightmare was so unreal she was not sure any more what was true and what was not. One thing she did know and that was that she did not want to hear any more. She simply could not bear it. She stood up.

'Please leave.'

'I'm sorry, Mrs Leiston,' the man said. 'The next few weeks are likely to be pretty rough for you. There obviously will have to be an investigation. If we can clear things up, privately – and get the money back – then we won't need to involve the police and we'll be able to leave you alone. I'm sure you understand?'

Jill stared at him. Her mind felt so blurry she had not the faintest idea what he meant but it sounded like a threat.

'I need access to any relevant documents Hugo had at home,' James Wheatley continued. 'Bank accounts, that sort of thing. We need to check everything. Did he have a study at home? A computer?'

Numb and despairing, Jill led him wordlessly to the study they had shared and gestured to Hugo's computer on the second desk.

'Anything relevant will be there,' she told him, and watched for a moment as he settled down at the desk and turned on the computer. He soon became engrossed so Jill left him to it, returning zombie-like to the sitting room where she cleared away the tea things.

As she stood, washing up the mugs in the kitchen, the mist cleared for a moment and it felt as though some pieces of a nightmarish jigsaw puzzle were beginning to slot into place. If Hugo had been embezzling from the firm – though she could not imagine why he would, after all they were not short of money with two good salaries coming in – but if he had been, and he had been found out, then maybe suicide would seem the logical option to him. She could understand someone like Hugo feeling unbearable shame. Hugo embezzling, though – she found that incomprehensible.

She set the tea towel down and stared blindly out of the window. She found the whole thing incomprehensible, unbelievable, unreal. Well, she reflected, it could be worse. So long as this James Wheatley found what he was looking for, then there would be no need for the much worse intrusion that would inevitably result if the police were involved. She had seen such things on television and did not think she could cope with that – having to let the police into the study, answering questions, and watching them take away bags filled with papers and files, and Hugo's computer wrapped in police-labelled plastic.

In her imagination she could see uniformed police going up and down the front path with their booty, piling it into the back of a police van, nosy gawping people clustered by the gate, stopping to watch. Some would be from the press, shouting out questions to the police, and when they spotted her at the window, they would try to get her to say something. She went back to the tea mugs in the sink and scrubbed angrily at the tea stains. This way had to be for the best – but it was still horrid. And it was so hard to take it in. Hugo, an embezzler?

At last, James Wheatley came through to tell her he was finished.

'I shouldn't think we'll need to disturb you further,' he told her. 'I'm sorry…'

'Yes, I know,' Jill said wearily and showed him to the door.

'If there's anything we can do to help…' he began, but she waved him away. At that moment all she wanted was to be left alone and as the days passed, it soon became clear that she was to get her wish. James Wheatley's visit had made the neighbours whisper and it appeared that news of the reason for Hugo's suicide had leaked out. Jill was aware of disapproving glances where once there had been smiles. She noticed people crossing the road to avoid her, of a sudden cessation of phone calls from people who had been on their dinner party list for years, of a cooling in her welcome at local activities. She found that she was hurrying through her shopping trips, avoiding people's eyes.

She still could not believe it, but when Jill tried to tell one well-wisher, she was told bluntly, 'But you can never really *know* someone, can you?' It appeared that was true. Her placid contented life which had seemed almost boring in its ordinariness had been turned upside down.

The last straw, however, was the blaring caption to a tabloid story prominently displayed outside her local newsagent's a week later:

SUICIDE EMBEZZLER'S SECRET LOVE NEST

It was obvious who the story was about. As Jill stared in horror at the placard, the owner came out and apologised in some embarrassment.

'I'm sorry, Mrs Leiston… but you know…'

Jill turned on him in sudden fury as all the suppressed emotion of the previous days came pouring out.

'No! I do *not* know, don't you see? It seems I'm the last person on earth to know anything about my husband and what was going on! So I'd better have one of your horrid newspapers and find out.'

Hands trembling, she found the coins to pay for the paper, shoved it into her bag and almost ran for her car. She forced herself to drive home, make herself a mug of coffee and sit down at the kitchen table before she read it.

There, in lurid detail, it related that Hugo had been having an affair with a secretary from the Birmingham firm, whom he had met during the run-up to the take-over. He had rented a flat in Bath as a secret hide-away where they could meet. It seemed that several of those 'meetings' in Birmingham had simply been a cover for his extra-marital activities. It also appeared that he had opened a bank account in Birmingham for the proceeds of his embezzlement which he had used to fund his secret lifestyle. Brochures left in the flat suggested he and the secretary were planning to leave the country.

There was a photograph of the mistress, Ms Sylvia Schafer. She looked rather hard, with a smoker's wrinkles and obviously dyed hair. Jill knew she was being bitchy but she could not help it. There was a picture of the flat too, with an open wardrobe showing Hugo had moved some of his clothes there so this was demonstrably no one-night stand but a significant commitment.

Jill stared at the newspaper article until the words blurred in front of her eyes. She had told the man from Hugo's firm that she did not believe Hugo had been involved in anything illegal. Now she was presented, in black and white, with what, to her, was much worse.

The company's financial affairs, she knew, were complicated. Russett & Thomson was a much-respected art and antiques auction house, with money moving around here, there and everywhere, every day. When she had calmed down after James Wheatley's visit and thought about his revelations of Hugo's embezzlement, she had hoped it would be discovered that Hugo had maybe made a mistake, misunderstood some new legal requirement, EU regulation or something, completely accidentally. Knowing Hugo as she had thought she did, she had convinced herself, despite everything James had said, that everything could be explained perfectly simply.

But this – she stared blindly at the tabloid pictures – this was a personal betrayal. A public slap in the face. And as she looked again at the older, hard face of the woman Hugo had chosen to be his mistress, the woman whom he had preferred to her and risked his career and reputation for, Jill felt sick and humiliated. She had thought he loved her. She had accepted his compliments as sincere. She had believed he was proud of her achievements as head teacher of the local primary school, that he was happy with how she looked and dressed.

She found herself walking out into the hall and standing in front of the long mirror there, assessing what she saw. Haunted dark eyes stared out of a pinched white shocked face. Her naturally dark hair was a mess and there was grey showing through. She was wearing a baggy old sweater and ancient jeans.

She knew she was not looking her best but then, she had never been that interested in clothes and make-up and jewellery. That was something Hugo had said he liked about her – that there was no fuss about her. That she could get ready to go out in remarkably few minutes. That she shopped for clothes like a man – knowing what she wanted and making swift decisions, instead of 'wasting hours like a silly bimbo window shopping'. He had praised her preference for comfort over fashion – clothes you could move in, shoes you could walk in.

The memories tumbled over one another. Shaking, Jill took herself back into the kitchen and gulped down the cooling coffee. Barney came over to comfort her but stroking his thick wiry fur did not seem to help. She found herself staring at the newspaper pictures again. Had Hugo been lying to her – everything he had said – not meaning a word of it?

It was as if she had never really known him. The man she had thought Hugo to be, for all those years, seemed to have been someone quite other. As she looked at the picture of the woman he had chosen instead of her, she wondered to herself, as she felt something, deep inside her, simply snap, do hearts really break?

The phone rang, jolting her out of the numb despair that overwhelmed her.

It was her mother, who lived in Bath near Jill's sister, Kay.

'Did you know about this?' her mother demanded.

'You've seen the newspaper?' Jill responded wearily.

'Hasn't everyone?' her mother retorted.

'I should think so,' Jill agreed unhappily. She had not thought about that.

'Well,' her mother prodded. 'Did you know?'

'No, Mum, I didn't. I didn't have any idea.' It came out as flat as Jill was feeling.

'Well, you're better off without him, then. That's what I say,' her mother concluded robustly before dissolving into a fit of coughing.

'Mum, are you all right? I thought you were going to get that cough seen to?'

'I was. But this seems more important.'

'Mum, please. I shall be all right. I'll manage, somehow. But you do need to see the doctor…'

It took a bit of persuading but finally Jill's 83-year-old mother agreed she would get Jill's sister to take her to the doctor's to get the cough checked out. They parted affectionately, bringing tears to Jill's eyes. What she really needed, she thought, was a hug. But Hugo was gone. She was a widow, and a betrayed one at that. There would be no more hugs…

As the bleakness threatened to overwhelm her, the phone rang again: first one friend, then another. It appeared that her mother had been correct. Everyone had seen the offending tabloid headline and devoured the article and the accompanying pictures. Some of the calls were supportive, others avid for gossip, still others maliciously gleeful.

'Gosh, Jill, how can you ever go out again?'

'My dear, it's a disgrace! We simply won't discuss it. How are you coping?'

'What a slag! What on earth did Hugo think he was doing?'

'It makes no difference to our friendship, whether it's true or not!'

But it did make a difference to the reception Jill got when she next ventured into the centre of town. There seemed to be whispering groups in every shop, darting sharp glances at her, and then turning their backs to continue their gossiping, uncaring that she knew who they were talking about. Where once she had been a respected and even popular local head teacher, with parents eager and proud to chat to her about their children, she was now an object of scandal, even disgrace. It took all her courage to complete the tasks she had set herself – greengrocer, baker, mini supermarket – and then to walk at her usual pace back to her car, when all she wanted to do was run for cover.

When she got home, there was a phone call from Jenneva Rawlings who lived on a farm on the outskirts of a nearby village.

'I saw you in the town just as I was leaving, and I saw the old biddies staring at you and gossiping. I just wanted to say: don't you mind them. I know what it's like to be the centre of nasty attention – don't I just! – but I promise you, if you'll just sit it out, it will all blow over.'

'Oh, I wish it would!' Jill told her fervently, thinking how kind it was of Jenneva to ring. They were not close friends – acquaintances more like, brought together many years back when Jenneva had brought her son to the entrance class at Jill's school. Jill had liked her instantly, though she knew Jenn had a murky past that had been the talk of the county. She was reputed to have a pretty murky present too. Now she had joined Jenn as the object of gossip, she realised. Of all the people she knew, Jenneva Rawlings was the one who would best understand what she was going through. It was an enormous relief and Jill found herself pouring it all out.

'And then – the firm's holding an investigation, and then there's the inquest and…' Jill's voice failed.

'Damn all men, that's what I say! Love 'em and leave 'em, that's the way. No point taking them seriously. You just get hurt. Look, love, I'm here if you need me. We women have to stick together! I'll even come to the inquest with you if you need me. Give you a bit of immoral support!' and Jenneva rang off, leaving Jill laughing despite herself.

Love 'em and leave 'em? She knew that was what the talk about Jenneva suggested, but it had never been her way. She had met Hugo at University and they had married quite young. There had never been anyone else for her and she had thought it had been the same for Hugo. They had always been happy together, even when they found they could not have the children they so longed for. Somehow, they had stuck together when their friends' marriages were falling apart. Somehow, they had pulled through and, she had thought, they had been looking forward to enjoying life even more after retirement. In fact, she had chosen to take early retirement the following spring to coincide with Hugo's sixty-fifth birthday, so that they could have more precious time together. They had been planning to move to a beautiful cottage in the village where Monica and Geoffrey lived, planning all sorts of lovely things…

Damn all men – even her beloved Hugo? The tears welled up and overflowed. And then the terrible pain surged through her chest in savage physicality. She wanted to crouch over and wrap her arms round and round herself, like the rings on a barrel, to hold herself in, but she knew, somehow, it would just make it worse. So she dragged herself up straight and found herself digging her nails into her chest, as if she were digging into her breastbone and tearing her flesh apart and open, wide enough to let the terrible pain out. As it etched its acid way through heart and soul and mind, she wondered how long she could endure this – and how much more she would have to suffer.

It finally drove her to her doctor, another old friend, who treated her with gentleness and understanding. No drugs. Just time off from work. Three months. And when she told the school that she had loved and nurtured for so many years, she was horrified to see how relieved they were. It was clear that she had become an embarrassing liability.

'You were planning early retirement,' she was told. 'Why don't you just let this three months' sick leave slide into that? I'm sure we can arrange things.' And they did, quickly and ruthlessly. Her friend, Monica, currently Deputy Head at another primary school, had hoped to take over when Jill retired so it was a bittersweet pleasure for Jill to see her friend move effortlessly into her place.

Jill had cleared the personal things from her desk, then gone home and wept bitter tears, but this time with anger – at Hugo. How could he have destroyed her life like this? Everything was gone – everything she loved: the school, her social life amongst people they had called friends....

She grabbed the phone and rang Eleanor, the minister of the group of churches where she helped out as a lay preacher.

'Do you want me to stop taking services? Am I *persona non grata* with you too?' she demanded.

'Don't be silly,' Eleanor's bracing tones reassured her. 'But maybe you need some time to get over this a bit.'

'Oh, no! Not you too! Just tell me straight you don't want me around to pollute your precious churches with my sullied reputation!'

Eleanor continued forcefully, 'I am not saying this to get rid of you. I'm not in the slightest bit embarrassed by any of this – nor are any of your real friends. None of it is about *you*! You just need some time to grieve and heal, then when you're ready, you tell me when you want to start leading worship again and that's what you'll do. Agreed?'

'Agreed,' Jill breathed out loudly with relief. Eleanor's definite tones had convinced her. 'OK. I'll take some time off, then.' She felt lighter. At least that had not been taken away from her. Her ministry maybe was on hold, but it was not permanent.

And somehow, having her diary cleared for her felt like a holiday. She could potter around the house, read, even watch television in the daytime. Eat as and when she fancied. She could sleep when she wanted to and for as long as she wanted.

And sleep was something she did a lot of, though she would often wake in the middle of the night and agonise over what she now knew about Hugo and wonder how she could have been so blind. The photographs in the tabloid hurt the most – black and white evidence that could not be avoided.

She found she could not help running them through her mind over and over again. That dreadful woman and that tawdry love nest! In her mind's eye she could see the wardrobe and Hugo's shirts hung up there, including the check one that was his favourite. Funny, he had been asking about that just the other week. She remembered she had told him if it was not in his wardrobe, it must be in the wash, and so he had gone back upstairs and chosen something else to wear. Shouldn't he have remembered he had taken it to Bath?

Jill sighed. She did not understand anything about it, and on that thought slipped back into sleep.

CHAPTER 4

❦

She had fed Barney and was making her own breakfast when the phone rang.

'Hi, I heard the news from Eleanor.' Liz was an old schoolfriend of Eleanor's who came regularly from her south-coast home to visit. She had been widowed the previous summer. 'Having been there, done that, got the t-shirt so to speak, can I offer a little advice – the kind I wish someone had given me?'

'Any help will be welcome,' Jill told her. 'It all feels like a nightmare. None of it seems real.'

'Well, first of all,' Liz said firmly 'that's normal. So don't think you're losing your marbles. It just feels like that for a while. It's one of the ways the body protects itself – sort of natural opiates that blur everything till you can cope again.'

'Blur!' Jill exclaimed. 'You can say that again. I feel as if I'm going around in a fog. I just can't seem to get my head round anything…'

'Have you been worrying about your memory – finding yourself going into a room and not knowing why you're there?'

'All the time!' Jill responded. 'And I find half-drunk mugs of cold coffee that I've completely forgotten about all over the place.'

'Right. Well, that's temporary too, honest! It will sort itself out and your memory will be fine again. It just takes time.'

'That *is* a relief! I really thought I was sinking prematurely into old age!'

'No way!' And Liz proceeded to share her hard-won wisdom, widow to widow, reassuring Jill that her reactions were normal. The final gem, however, came as an unwelcome shock.

'We're vulnerable, you see. A certain type of man tends to think that if we've been happily married for a number of years, we'll be missing the regular sex and physical contact. As a result we may be a bit desperate and … well, easy. So be ready for a few embarrassing situations. Even some of the men you thought were nice and firmly married and completely safe will try it on.'

'So what am I meant to do? Put myself in purdah?' Jill asked indignantly.

'No, no!' Liz laughed. 'And you don't have to dress like a nun and behave like a Puritan, either, but it's something you need to be aware of so you can deal with it gently!'

Jill was outraged. 'Gently? What I'd like to do if anyone tried it on me…'

'Yes, I know, but it's better to leave the poor fellow his pride!'

Jill snorted.

'Give it time,' Liz soothed. 'I know everyone will tell you that, but time does make the difference.'

Time? Each day it seemed such an effort just to get up and do the everyday things, plodding one foot after the other through the hours till she could go to bed again. Even her morning session of prayer and Bible reading which she used to so enjoy seemed now to take an effort. Her journal where she wrote her prayers and the thoughts that came to her from the reading remained blank, day after day. There seemed to be nothing to say. Life was on hold till the inquest.

It was held in the imposing Shire Hall in Taunton, a cross between a castle and a cathedral with every possible Gothic decoration fitted in somewhere, but still inside, in the waiting room, there was that inescapable institutional smell and uncomfortable chairs to sit on. Jenneva Rawlings, true to her word, had arrived in her mud-spattered Range Rover to take Jill to the inquest and now ushered her protectively into the room where little groups of people stood or sat in awkward silence, not looking at one another. Geoffrey Harris, there as Jill's solicitor, stopped by awkwardly with words intended to comfort but Jill felt like a zombie and simply sat where she was told and waited till it was time to move. Even with Jenneva at her side, she felt naked and vulnerable – the widow, the one Hugo had dumped for the mistress and the love nest in Bath. She felt she was being watched in an unfriendly way as she waited, and she felt herself shrink inside herself.

The actual room was like a courtroom and she was called as a witness, though she had little enough to contribute. She felt foolish and ashamed to have been so ignorant, so unaware of what had been going on. She wondered if she was imagining disbelief in the coroner's reactions to her pathetic answers of 'I'm sorry, I don't know anything about that… I didn't know… I don't know' until she was close to tears.

James Wheatley was there, elegant in a charcoal-grey suit and dark tie, giving evidence on behalf of the firm. There seemed to be a lot of technical detail about the embezzled money. Now they had located the bank account, the firm were prepared to draw a line under Hugo's criminal activities.

When Sylvia Schafer was called, Jill was shocked not to have realised she would be there, and she found herself staring.

The woman was older than Jill had expected, significantly older than herself, but very elegant in a beautifully cut dark grey coat with a fine silk scarf in toning shades of grey and blue at her throat. Thin legs were clad in fine sheer dark nylon and her shoes were fashionable and smart. Her hair, dismissed by Jill from the photographs as dyed, was now seen to have benefited from expensive highlights giving an impression of ash blonde. She wore pearl and gold earrings, discreet make-up that highlighted smoky eyes, and her voice, when she gave her evidence, matched.

'Whisky and cigarettes,' Jenneva leaned over and whispered bitchily.

Jill, hands clenched into fists inside her pockets, listened with horrified fascination as the woman described her relationship with Hugo.

'Yes, I loved him,' she declared in a husky voice. 'He said his marriage had reached the point of no return some time ago. He had been planning to separate from his wife when he retired. We were planning...' She dabbed at her eyes with a small lace-edged handkerchief.

'Go on, Miss Schafer,' the coroner instructed gravely.

She swallowed and went on, 'We were planning to move to Spain together – a new life in the sun!' A wan smile faded and the handkerchief dabbed again.

Finally all the evidence had been given, the coroner recorded a verdict of suicide and the court emptied. But Jill remained sitting, stunned. Then suddenly she erupted.

'Our marriage had broken down some time ago! Surely I'd have known something about that? I'm not stupid!'

'Let's get out of here,' Jenneva said, taking Jill's arm to try to lead her away before they attracted unwanted attention. But Jill shook her off.

'And Hugo was planning to leave me for a new life in Spain? He'd have hated that. Oh, that horrid woman! She must have talked him into it. But he'd have absolutely hated it! He wouldn't ever go abroad. He said he didn't see the point of all that travelling just to start your holiday exhausted when everything he ever wanted was here in England... All our holidays had to be in England just because he wouldn't go abroad! No matter how I moaned, it had to be Swanage, or Cornwall or…'

'Come *on*!' Jenneva tugged her arm.

'That… that harpy!' Jill ground out through her teeth. She was shaking with fury.

'That's putting it mildly,' Jenneva agreed, as she guided her down the stairs to the Range Rover.

In the car park, a cluster of people stood smoking and taking gulps from mineral water bottles beside a sleek black Jaguar. Sylvia Schafer was amongst them.

'Huh,' Jenneva snorted as she hurried Jill past. 'Mineral water! Who are they kidding? I got Frank to bring me whisky and red wine in a couple of those last time I was in hospital. The nurses didn't spot anything through the green plastic. Well, I think we both deserve a proper drink. Let's go!'

She shovelled a now unresisting Jill into the Range Rover and sped off. The pleasant country pub she found was not too far away but after a swift brandy, all Jill wanted to do was to get home and, like a wounded animal, lick her wounds in private. Her outburst had exhausted her.

Before she left her, Jenneva reminded Jill that the coroner had released Hugo's body so Jill's next task was to arrange the funeral.

'Funeral?' Jill exclaimed in horror. 'Oh no! *She'll* want to come! Jenn, how can I stop her! I couldn't bear it…'

'Well, you know I'm not into church and all that. Do you have to have a church funeral?'

Jill stared at her in confusion. Jenneva explained: 'If you do, then it's a public place and it's open to anyone – so you can't stop the witch coming. But say you decided on a nice private cremation, by invitation only… You can do that, you know. Put it in the paper at the end of the death notice. You know where they say, "Family flowers only"? Put "Private cremation, by invitation only". And you can still have your minister to do the service… just like you'd have had at church. That would be a way round it.'

'That sounds good,' Jill said with relief. 'Yes, Hugo would have wanted to be cremated anyway…' Jill turned to her with a sudden smile. 'Jenneva, you're a genius! That's what I'll do – and then Miss Sylvia Bloody Schafer won't be able to come anywhere near us!'

Jenneva choked. She had never heard Jill, whom she had always thought of as a quiet and rather proper teacher/preacher lady use such language, but maybe it was good for her to start expressing her feelings.

The anger kept Jill going through the interview with the kindly undertaker and the shock of the price of a cremation. Luckily, Hugo's life insurance policy had not contained a suicide clause and had been written in trust for Jill so she felt confident about covering the various costs.

One question threw her though.

'And what would you like to do with the ashes, Mrs Leiston?'

Oh yes, the ashes.

'I have a choice?' Jill found herself asking stupidly.

'Yes, of course. You can have them interred in the Garden of Rest at the crematorium – it's a very pretty rose garden – and we can arrange for a nice plaque to be put in the encircling wall. Or perhaps your local churchyard might have some space? On the other hand, you might wish to do something different – scattering the ashes somewhere special?'

'I'd throw him off Glastonbury Tor if I could, alive. See how he felt then!' Jill thought fiercely, but instead she replied, 'I'm afraid I'm not really sure what I would like to do. Do I have to make up my mind now?'

'No, no,' she was assured. 'You just take your time. You can always keep the ashes at home for a little while…'

And that reminded her of a dear friend who kept her husband's ashes on her bedroom mantelpiece, waiting for when her ashes would be able to join his in one grave. Jill smiled. That's what she would do. She would put Hugo's ashes on the mantelpiece and then she could yell at him as she had never done in their life together and tell him exactly what she thought of him and his illegal activities and his slaggy Miss Sylvia Schafer. And then she would decide what to do with them – maybe even put him out in the rubbish where he belonged

Calmly, she responded to the undertaker, 'Yes, I think that's what I'll do – till I decide… Now, can I get you another cup of tea?'

CHAPTER 5

❈

THE DAY OF the funeral was another beautiful autumn morning, crisp, with a touch of frost. Jenneva, who seemed to have taken on the role of fierce protector, drove Jill to the crematorium at Taunton where they met minister Eleanor, Jill's sister Kay and her husband Peter, and a few carefully chosen friends including Monica and Geoffrey.

As Jill tried to sing the words of the hymns she had chosen, her voice broke. She realised she simply could not sing. It was not grief, it was just the meaninglessness of it all. She should have been saying goodbye to someone she loved, but here she was going through the motions for someone she felt she no longer knew. It was a double loss and she felt desolate.

Eleanor moved smoothly through the service, her voice calming and kind. And then came the moment when the coffin moved through the opened curtains, and the curtains closed behind it. This was finality. Hugo's body would be cremated. Hugo was no more, gone far beyond her reach, far beyond the questions Jill ached to ask, the screaming outrage she longed to unleash. She sighed. *Finis.* She would never know the truth of it all, this horrid mess that had taken her life and smashed it beyond recognition.

Later she was aware that she had gone home, that there had been tea – and some brandy – along with something to eat, but she could not remember what it was. Sandwiches, maybe? She remembered wandering vaguely into the kitchen where her sister and friends were doing the washing-up and how the conversation had stopped, cut in its tracks by her appearance. She had stood there, feeling like the Ancient Mariner in her own house, Hugo's death and all the scandal surrounding it the smelly rotting albatross round her neck.

They had fussed and put her to bed before they left. And then, when they had all gone, Jill had got up again, feeling like a naughty child, and wandered round the house, opening cupboards and touching things. Smelling flowers. Petting Barney. Trying to reassure herself that some things had not changed and that she was still alive.

When she got up next morning and went to her desk for her morning devotions, she found her journal was open and written there in a terrible scrawl were the words: 'When you took your life, you took mine too. Now your body's been cremated, but mine remains, undead but no longer truly alive.'

A few days later, Hugo's ashes arrived. Monica had been in Taunton for a meeting – the kind of meeting of head teachers that Jill used to spend so much of her time at and complain was such a waste of time – and she had collected the ashes from the crematorium and brought them to Jill. After some thought Jill put the shiny white plastic urn in the centre of her bedroom mantelpiece and looked at it.

It did not mean anything. It was not Hugo in there. Hugo was gone – gone from the moment the deception had started, the moment the affair with Sylvia Schafer had begun. So yes, she could cope with having the plastic urn there. There was something honest about it in its very plastic tawdriness that summed up the shameful ending to a life that she would have expected to have been very different. A decent funeral at the least, for such a pillar of the community. A fine wooden coffin with shiny brass handles. Masses of flowers. Soaring organ music and maybe an anthem from the choir. The great and good from all the committees that Hugo had sat on or chaired, people from the firm…

A picture flashed into her mind of the meticulously turned-out Miss Sylvia Schafer at the inquest, dabbing her eyes with the little lace-edged handkerchief that never seemed to smudge her carefully applied eye make-up.

No. Don't go there.

Jill looked at the cheap plastic urn. Yes, that was all her beloved Hugo was worth now. Dust and ashes in a cheap plastic urn.

She was taken aback when a messenger from the firm arrived at her door, bringing her a collection of items, including a bagful of the various articles belonging to Hugo which had been returned from the flat in Bath by the letting agents. Distressed, she did not want to touch them but then curiosity got the better of her and she tipped the bag out onto the sitting room floor and picked over the items, gently pushing a nosy Barney out of the way.

There was Hugo's favourite check shirt. A bit faded and worn soft, but still his favourite. It did not smell like him though. There was none of the faint traces of pipe smoke that somehow always lingered to scent his clothes. She supposed it had hung in the wardrobe in Bath long enough after his death for the scent to have faded. A couple of other unfamiliar shirts looked barely out of their packaging. She supposed he had bought them new for his new life. The two pairs of underpants were familiar, as were the socks. And there was a pair of grey trousers she had thought were at the cleaners.

The rest of the things were a strange collection of odds and ends. An old alarm clock – the last she had seen of that was at the back of a drawer. Hugo had kept it as a fall-back after she had bought him the new clock-radio he had wanted for Christmas. There was an unfamiliar toilet bag and a few toiletries – the shaving cream he liked, a couple of throw-away razors, the deodorant he always used.

Surprisingly, there were no books – but maybe he had better things to do with his time with Miss Schafer than read, Jill thought with sudden bitterness, as she recalled the evenings they had spent in front of a roaring log fire, classical music playing in the background, sitting reading, she had thought, peacefully and contentedly.

She realised that what she had been afraid of finding was some evidence of that woman – but there was no scent, no trace of perfume, no silent witness to Hugo's perfidy, simply returned items that smelt and felt strangely neutral, as if they had simply been in store for a while.

Sighing she got up to sort out places for the things. As she hung the shirt back in Hugo's wardrobe, she chided herself that it was past time she packed up all his clothes and gave them away to charity. But then a gentle waft of what she always thought of as the Hugo smell – male, fragrant with pipe smoke – drifted from the clothes in front of her and she found herself burying her face in his old tweed jacket and weeping, helplessly and hopelessly.

She did not understand what had happened and she did not think she ever could. She had thought they were perfectly happy, perfectly comfortable together. Maybe that was it? Maybe they had been too comfortable and Hugo had got bored? But she had not thought he was the type of man who got bored. He preferred settled ways and familiar things, like this battered old tweed jacket, well past its best, the worn soft favourite shirt, his home, his wife…

Eleanor's friend Liz had told her it only *felt* like she was losing her marbles – but Jill sometimes felt on the edge of succumbing completely to such a fit of the screaming heebie-jeebies that they would need heavy machinery and frogmen to dig her out. She could sense the temptation just on the edge of her mind, beckoning. A black, black place she could plunge screaming into and never come out.

Gently patting the jacket and shirts back into place, she drew herself unsteadily out of the wardrobe. As she left the room, she gave the urn on the mantelpiece a dirty look.

'It's all your fault,' she told Hugo. 'And you've left me to pick up the pieces. That's just not fair!'

Downstairs, as she went to make herself a restorative mug of coffee, the phone rang.

'James Wheatley,' a velvety voice said. 'I hope I'm not disturbing you?'

Shock silenced her. Why would he ring her now? Wasn't everything wound up now the inquest was over, the funeral past?

'You do remember me?' he asked into the silence.

Jill swallowed hard. How could she forget the bearer of such bad news? It seemed the nightmare had only really begun when James turned up.

'I saw you at the inquest,' he continued. 'What a horrid thing to have to sit through. I believe the funeral was on Thursday?'

Jill acknowledged this, wondering what he wanted now. Surely the firm were satisfied now they had sorted it all out?

'Look, I'm going to be down in your neck of the woods next week and wondered… I've got an evening viewing at the Ilminster auction rooms on Wednesday evening and thought – I don't have to get back to Birmingham. I've taken a little flat in Yeovil for when I need to stay over. Anyway, I was wondering if I could take you out for supper afterwards, somewhere nice. Cheer you up a bit.'

Jill was surprised. This was unexpected kindness. A little outing would be a treat. Liz's warnings echoed in the recesses of her mind but she waved them away. All the usual invitations that used to comprise her social life had dried up, so maybe a meal out some place nice with someone who understood her situation would indeed brighten up her life. She realised she had become very isolated. So many of their erstwhile friends were giving her the cold shoulder, she almost felt that she had been sent to Coventry locally. Without the busy daily routine of school, she was beginning to feel very much at a loose end. If she were now *persona non grata* and tarred with the same brush as Hugo, then she really did not have anything to lose. She knew how Jenneva would react: with total warm encouragement. For a moment Jill hesitated, then she took the plunge.

'Why not?' she replied, as the frisson of doing something that felt slightly naughty lifted her spirits.

'I am delighted,' the voice purred, and he did indeed seem delighted. 'If I may, I'll call for you at about eight o'clock…'

As she put the phone down after agreeing to the arrangements he suggested, she found herself wondering what she could wear. Black, of course. But a wisp of mischief tweaked her mouth. Black suited her. Wasn't that fortunate?

CHAPTER 6

❈

It had been a long time since Jill had taken any real trouble over her appearance but since she had time on her hands and a surprise outing to look forward to, it was rather fun to go shopping for something nice to wear. She felt like a schoolgirl again. And like a naughty schoolgirl, she decided not to mention her plans to Monica, her head-teacher – and church – friend. Instead she turned to Jenneva Rawlings whom she knew would understand and support her.

Jenneva jumped at the opportunity of a day's shopping with Jill. She was also predictably enthusiastic about the dinner engagement with James.

'I must admit I thought he was quite dishy when I saw him at the inquest,' she confessed. 'Good for you. Time to get your own back. After all, what's sauce for the goose… or in this case the other way round!'

When Jill explained that the reason for a shopping spree was that she felt in need of something new to wear for the dinner, Jenn told her robustly, 'Apart from your teachery/

preachery clothes, all I've ever seen you in are jeans so I reckon it's past time you treated yourself to something new and sexy!'

Jill laughed at Jenneva's succinct summation of her wardrobe and reminded her, 'It's got to be black. I'm keeping to black.'

'He doesn't deserve it,' Jenn muttered darkly. Her steadfast support did not extend to Hugo whom she considered had unforgivably let Jill down.

Jill found herself in surprisingly high spirits and she responded gaily, 'Don't you worry! I promise you I'll buy myself a red dress when I get over this and feel really happy again!'

'I'll hold you to that!' Jenn told her and the two of them laughed and set off from the car park to the shops.

They had chosen Yeovil for the excursion and soon found 'the dress' in an exclusive boutique. Black, admittedly, but with a deep scoop neck 'to make the most of your assets', as Jenn put it. It had tiny black buttons up the front, long sleeves, and a full skirt that flared from a neatly fitted bodice. All in all, very flattering.

'New earrings?'

That led to a glorious browse which produced a fine pair of silver earrings from a small craft shop. They were beautifully designed and hand-made, with an intricate Celtic border around a shining black enamel centre.

As Jill tried them on, she remembered the flashy gold and pearl earrings Miss Sylvia Schafer had worn to the inquest. Gold did not suit Jill – she always wore silver – and with a pang she remembered Hugo teasing her that she was a 'cheap date', not being greedy for gold and 'jools' as he laughingly called them. Looking at the price of the silver earrings – they were expensive – she was stung by the memory. So she had been cheap. Well, it did not look like Sylvia Schafer had been if Hugo had needed to embezzle from the firm to keep her. Rebelliously, Jill pulled out her credit card and paid quickly before her instinctive thriftiness could rise up and stop her.

Tea in a cosy tearoom close to the car park and a thorough trawl round the nearby supermarket finished off the trip.

'This is such a relief,' Jill told Jenneva. 'I've been feeling so uncomfortable shopping locally. I feel as though everyone's staring and whispering about me. It's horrible. Makes me want to hide.'

'It will all blow over,' Jenn reassured her. 'Something else will take their interest and they'll forget all about you. Just keep your head down for a while and it will go away.'

'I don't know,' Jill said. 'Small places tend to have long memories. And even though it wasn't me who did anything wrong, there's always the old "no smoke without fire" thing. If I can hardly believe that I didn't know anything was going on, how can I expect anyone else to believe me?'

'Your real friends believe you,' Jenn said. 'People who know you – they know you're telling the truth, because you're that kind of person.'

'I suppose so,' Jill said slowly. 'Truth has always been important to me. Without truth there's really nothing you can rely on.'

They loaded their bags of shopping into Jenn's Range Rover and drove back to Jill's house. As she helped Jill carry the bags to her door, Jenn said thoughtfully, 'It's funny though. You'd have thought you would have known – but I suppose he'd have had to be secretive about it all. I suppose like I am, so poor old Frank doesn't know what I'm up to. I've always thought that what he didn't know couldn't hurt him – but now I'm not so sure.' She gave Jill a fierce hug and muttered, 'I could kill your Hugo!'

Jill laughed, though she had tears in her eyes. 'Too late!' she said. 'Someone got there before you.'

As she went into the house, Jill recalled what she had said. She had meant Hugo himself, of course, but now she thought about it, that did not ring true. Suicide just was not his way of dealing with things. He would always confront situations head on, even if it meant coming out of it with a bloody nose. She remembered the arguments he had been involved in on committees, fighting for the rights of villagers against developers and such like. Even when it turned out he was on the losing side, Hugo did not just lie down and give up. And Jill, who preferred a quiet life, had often wished he would. But it just was not in his nature.

Yet the coroner had said it was suicide. Jill had seen Hugo's body herself. He was truly dead, she knew that. The ashes were in that dreadful plastic urn on her bedroom mantelpiece. But had he really killed himself?

She plonked her shopping down on the kitchen counter. What on earth was she thinking about? This was ridiculous. They had had the inquest, the police had had their say, and the firm too. The verdict had been suicide. Maybe she was losing her marbles after all.

'What do you think, Barney?' she asked the cat. Getting no reply, she went to make herself a mug of coffee while she put the shopping away.

Jill managed to surprise her hairdresser by turning up for a trim and blow-dry sooner than her usual once-every-two-months utility visit which was necessary simply to keep her hair under control and relatively respectable. Even more out of character was her request for something 'a little different'. Everyone at the salon had obviously heard about Hugo's death and the scandal surrounding it, but after a few curious glances, they simply left Jill to relax into having her hair washed, trimmed and styled.

Lulu, her stylist for many years, was kind and discreet, offering her condolences and hoping that Jill was feeling better.

'A new hairstyle will cheer you up,' she said confidently.

And it did. When Jill saw the new, more feminine style in the mirror she was very pleased. She would not admit to herself that this make-over had anything to do with the horrid Miss Sylvia Schafer, but she was able to hold her head up a little higher as she left the salon, and her new-found confidence carried her back to her car without caring about the inquisitive looks or whispered gossip.

She even applied a little make-up and nail polish as she prepared for her 'little treat' as she had taken to calling it. Smiling at her reflection in the mirror, she was surprised to see that some sparkle had returned to her eyes. Yes, she was looking forward to having dinner out in the company of a personable man. Jenneva was right – James was quite dishy. Maybe she did deserve a little fun. And she thought back to the months before Hugo's death when she had been so absorbed with work. There had been the usual staffing shortages and the inevitable problems with the budget. She had thought Hugo had been just as absorbed in his work and all the extra things resulting from the take-over. She could see, looking back, that they had not had much time to have fun together then. Maybe that was when things started to go wrong and Hugo was tempted to stray.

At that point the phone rang and Jill's heart sank. With a sudden pang, she felt sure it would be James apologising that he had to call off their dinner. But it was her sister, Kay.

'Jill, Mum's been rushed into hospital. That rotten emphysema again.'

'Should I come?' Jill offered at once.

'No, no need for that. Well, I don't think so. I'm going back to the hospital now and I'll ring you if there's anything you need to know, or if you should come. Is that all right?'

'Yes, of course.' Then Jill remembered. 'Look, Kay, I'm going out tonight…'

'Oh, yes?' her sister queried with interest. 'What are you doing?'

'Oh, only dinner with a friend.' Jill tried to play down the little treat she had been so looking forward to.

'Really?' Kay replied. 'Male friend by any chance?'

'It's all perfectly innocent,' Jill told her crossly. 'He works for the firm Hugo did, took over Hugo's job in fact, and I think he feels a bit guilty, you know, so it's his way of compensating, being kind to the widow… It's very nice of him.' She knew she was trying to convince herself.

Kay however was not swayed. 'Mmm. Is he nice?'

'Yes, I think so. Not bad looking, nice voice…' She stopped, deciding it was wiser to play down the charms which had so captured Jenneva's attention.

'Well, good for you,' her sister declared. 'You deserve. Now, I suppose it's just possible you might go back to his place for coffee, right?' The tease was back in her voice.

'Oh, Kay, don't tease me! You know I never looked at another man but Hugo and it's all a bit daunting.'

'You'll be fine,' Kay reassured her. 'Now, do you happen to have a number for him just in case I need to get hold of you urgently?'

'Yes,' Jill said. 'He gave me his number in case I needed it.'

'Right. I've got that,' her sister said as Jill read out the number. 'I promise I won't use it unless I absolutely have to. I don't want to mess up your romantic evening!'

'Oh, Kay!'

'And don't forget: if you can't be good, be careful!' With a laugh, her sister hung up, leaving Jill suddenly uncertain and wondering just what she was doing, going out to dinner with a man she did not know so soon after Hugo's death.

She did not get very far in her thinking before the doorbell rang and James was ushering her into his beautiful black Jaguar. He complimented her on her appearance and then said, 'I thought we'd go to Little Barwick House. I don't know if you know it?'

'I've heard of it,' Jill said. 'But I haven't been there.'

'It's on the other side of Yeovil so it's a little way from here,' James said. 'It's nice and discreet so I thought you'd enjoy it. And the food is wonderful!'

He drove confidently through the winding narrow country lanes and finally into the drive to Little Barwick House. The Georgian house was a beacon of welcoming light in the darkness and once inside, log fires and a bottle of champagne soon thawed any ice.

Before long they were laughing like old friends and Jill found she was enjoying herself more than she had for ages. James was easy to talk to and she found she had told him all about her mother in hospital, her sister, and most of her lifestory before they had even started the meal.

James explained in his turn that he was separated.

'No, nobody around at the moment.'

There had been somebody but that had come to an end several months ago, so now he was 'fancy free' and his eyes danced as he said this. With a start, Jill realised that as a widow, she too was 'fancy free'. There were no hindrances to new… friendships. She did not want to think any further than that, but she had to admit she was enjoying herself.

She looked up to see James observing her as she thought her way through this new idea, then he smiled and lifted his glass to her.

'So that makes two of us,' he said.

Jill glugged back her wine to cover her embarrassment.

The dining room was a luxurious haven, with dark red walls, crisp white table linen and sparkling glassware. The food, as James promised, was excellent. There was gravadlax to start, which went well with the last of the champagne. Then a rich main course of guineafowl followed, with crisp golden baby roast potatoes and a selection of fresh vegetables from the garden.

Jill was delighted that James did not try to sway her when she explained, 'I really can't drink very tannic red wine. Even when I've only had one glass, I'm sure to have a savage headache the next day.'

'So what would you prefer?' he asked.

'I think I'd call it alcoholic Ribena,' she said. 'You know, very light and fruity.'

He laughed at her description and recommended a delightful Fleury which was just right.

To her surprise, Jill discovered she was hungry and she ate with pleasure. The conversation flowed. She found it pleasant to be the focus of such interested attention. Maybe she talked too much but James seemed to encourage her and it made such a nice change from being cooped up alone in the house with only Barney the cat and the radio or television for company. To her surprise, she found herself pouring out her thoughts about how busy she had been in the last weeks of Hugo's life.

'Maybe I didn't pay enough attention,' she said sadly. 'I was tearing in and out of the house to meetings and we barely had a chance to talk about anything. I wonder if I neglected him, gave him the reason for what happened…'

'I really don't think you should blame yourself,' James told her firmly. 'Some things we'll never know.' And he distracted her with the choice of dessert. Seeing her indecision, the cheerful young waitress offered a spoonful of each of the three Jill was trying to decide between, rather than forcing her to make a choice.

When they had finished their meal and Jill had drained the last drops of the Muscat dessert wine James had insisted she try with her pudding, he rose and held her chair for her, murmuring, 'It's getting a bit busy in here, isn't it?'

Jill had not really noticed. She had felt cocooned in their own corner but now that she looked around, she saw that every table was occupied.

'I wonder, maybe it would be better if you came back to my place for coffee?' James suggested. 'I think you'll find the lounge here is heaving.' And when they went past to get their coats, Jill saw it was busy with late diners drinking aperitifs before their meals and satisfied diners having coffee after theirs.

It was a quiet journey to James's flat on the northern outskirts of Yeovil. James seemed to be concentrating on his driving and Jill had to admit to herself that she was feeling just a little woozy from all the wine she had consumed. She was, she decided, also maybe a little light-headed from James's very flattering attention.

His flat was on the first floor of an Edwardian house, with ample parking at the side. Once James had opened the door and ushered her inside, he said, 'Would you excuse me a moment? I'll just put the kettle on and get rid of my coat.' He pushed open the door to a comfortably furnished sitting room saying, 'Go through and make yourself at home.'

Jill was glad of a moment to herself to gather her scattered wits. Remembering Liz's warning a little too late, she wondered if maybe she had wandered into the lion's den, coming to James's flat like this. But then she chided herself: what he had said had been perfectly true. The lounge at Little Barwick had been very crowded and she was not really ready to appear in public with a new escort so soon after Hugo's death. James was just being thoughtful.

She took a deep breath to calm what she decided were silly schoolgirl nerves and looked around the room, noting the squashy sofa and deep easy chairs ranged round the fire. A flashing red light drew her attention to an Answermachine on a side table. Sudden panic grabbed her. She had given James's telephone number to her sister and Kay had promised to ring only if she was needed urgently. Her mother must have taken a turn for the worse. That was one of the most frightening things for them all. For someone with emphysema, a cold could suddenly escalate into something life-threatening. Without thinking, she was across the room and pressing the button on the Answermachine, her heart pounding with fear as she waited for her sister's voice.

But it was a husky voice, a woman's voice, which said, 'Darling! It's me. Just ringing for a little chinwag to chew the fat. Call me when you get in, darling. I'll be home all evening. 'Bye.'

And then James erupted into the room. He grabbed Jill's arm with one hand and stabbed at the button on the Answermachine to stop the message with the other. His face was a mask of fury as he turned and shouted at her, 'You stupid bitch! What the hell do you think you're doing?'

Jill froze. No one had ever spoken to her like that before. Then anger came to her rescue and she wrenched her arm away.

'I thought it would be my sister!' she protested. 'Remember, I told you about my mother – she's been taken into hospital – and my sister needed a contact number in case she took a turn for the worse and I had to get there in a hurry – so I gave her your number and when I saw the light flashing, I thought something had happened…'

Jill could hear herself babbling but James's fury had frightened her. Maybe if she went on talking he would calm down and then she could make an excuse and get away from there.

'My mother's got emphysema and it's very unpredictable.' She kept going doggedly. 'It's caused by smoking, of course. Mum was one of those people who started smoking during the war and she's never been able to stop. Hugo absolutely hated it. He despised cigarette smokers even though he occasionally smoked a pipe himself, but only outside the house…' Jill tailed off helplessly. 'Well anyway, as I said, I gave my sister your number – for emergency use only…'

'Oh, you poor thing.' The fury had gone from James's face and he seemed completely under control as he spoke in his normal urbane tone. 'You must have been so worried. Look, why don't I get you a brandy to go with your coffee…'

In just a few moments, James had gone from Jekyll to Hyde and then back again to the charming considerate man she had had dinner with. In fact, he was behaving as if nothing had happened. But Jill did not feel safe any more. She had glimpsed something of the man underneath that smooth charming manner and she no longer trusted herself with him one bit.

She managed to say 'No, I don't think so' as she sat down on the edge of one of the easy chairs, and added with a little unnatural laugh, 'I think I've had enough to drink tonight. Just coffee will be great.'

Without another word, he brought through a tray – set with a cafetière, two pretty porcelain mugs and a jug of milk, a tiny sugar bowl and a saucer of petits fours – and sat down on the sofa to pour the coffee.

'How very civilised,' Jill complimented him. 'In my house, all you get is a mug of instant.' But she knew the tray had to have been prepared in advance. Instead of feeling flattered as she would have been only ten minutes ago, now she felt very like a fly in a spider's web.

She sipped her coffee and tried to think calmly. How could she get home? Could she find a taxi? As the silence began to lengthen uncomfortably between them, she scrabbled for suitable safe conversational topics. As a thought crossed her mind, she found herself blurting out, 'The lady who left you the message… I thought you said you were fancy free but she sounded rather friendly?'

Once it was out Jill cringed. The alcohol had clearly loosened her inhibitions more than she realised. But surprisingly James did not seem to mind. He replied smoothly, 'Oh, that's just a friend. She's heavily into the theatre and all that. You know how they call everyone "darling". It doesn't mean a thing. Now, why don't you come over here.' James patted the sofa beside him. 'You're a long way away.'

'I don't think so,' Jill said quietly. 'In fact, I'm beginning to feel rather sleepy and should like to go home now.' She set down her coffee mug, stood up and offered James her hand. 'It's been a lovely evening. Thank you so much for taking pity on me. I do appreciate your kindness.'

He seemed surprised but duly put down his coffee mug and rose to take the proffered hand. Holding on to it rather longer than felt comfortable for Jill who had to steel herself not to wrench it away and make a run for the door, he smiled down into her eyes.

'I hoped you might see it as something a little more personal than kindness,' James murmured.

Jill tried to think of a suitable response but was overwhelmed by an enormous yawn.

'Oh, I'm terribly sorry!' she gasped. 'That was awfully rude of me. James, I just am so tired – I'm not used to going out to dinner so late, and I'm just not accustomed to so much rich food, not to mention all that lovely wine. Would you mind awfully taking me home – or ringing for a taxi?'

She thanked him again as she got out of his car at her door. Once safely indoors, she checked her own Answermachine and was glad to find no message from her sister.

Relief and exhaustion swept over her and she removed the new dress, the unfamiliar make-up, and the precious new earrings swiftly before she fell into bed. She was so glad to be safe, alone, in her own home. Her little treat had not turned out to be what she had hoped for.

In the middle of the night, she woke, uncomfortable with indigestion and desperately thirsty. Serve you right, she thought – all that food and far too much wine. She really was not used to it. Come to think of it, wine did not really agree with her that much at all.

As she climbed the stairs back to bed with a bottle of mineral water and a glass, it suddenly came to her where she had heard that husky voice on the Answermachine before. It was at the inquest and it was Miss Sylvia Schafer's, she was sure of it. The last time Jill had heard those smoky tones, the owner was dabbing her eyes with a handkerchief and declaring her love for Hugo. Strange that now she was phoning another man and calling him "darling"? But before Jill could ponder it further, sleep blotted everything out.

CHAPTER 7

❂

SHE WAS HAVING a late breakfast next morning and suffering. Even two paracetamols and a half-pint of ice-cold orange juice had not helped. She was seriously considering tomato juice laced with enough Tabasco to take the top of her head off and ease the pressure when the phone rang. Hanging on to her throbbing head, she struggled through to the hall and managed not to groan as she picked up the telephone.

'So how was it?' Jenneva Rawlings enquired cheerfully.

The groan escaped as Jill tried to sort out her muddled thoughts. Even thinking was painful.

'That good?' Jenn asked.

'Good?' Jill echoed in disbelief. 'Jenneva, I've got the mother of all headaches and I feel like death would be a blessing…'

'I see,' Jenn said soothingly. 'Just start at the beginning and take it gently.'

'Beginning? Can I even remember the beginning? We went to Little Barwick House. That much I'm sure of,' Jill told her.

'Little Barwick? Lucky you! He must have a few shillings in his pocket,' Jenneva said. 'And then?'

'We ate – the food was gorgeous – and drank… rather a lot, I think. Oh, my head!' she groaned again.

'Ah!' Jenn said thoughtfully. 'So he got you tanked up?'

Jill considered Jenneva's suggestion as seriously as the pain in her temples would let her. 'Looking back, I think it was quite a lot. The problem is that I'm just not used to it.'

'How much is quite a lot?' Jenn asked. 'Can you remember?'

'Well, I remember there was a bottle of champagne to start. That was rather nice. It helped to break the ice. Then there was a bottle of red with the main course. He was very nice about ordering something light that I'd like. I think I'd probably had enough by then but I kind of got persuaded to try a sweet wine to go with the pudding. It was delicious!'

'Sounds like quite the seduction scene,' Jenn commented. 'Right, what happened next – or were you legless at that point?'

'Of course not!' Jill protested indignantly. 'Well, maybe a bit woozy. We went back to his place for coffee. He said the lounge at the hotel was too busy and noisy.'

'Oh yes?'

'It was just coffee,' Jill insisted, then gave in. 'Well, all right, I reckon he may have been planning something more. The coffee tray was all beautifully set! I'm not sure what else he had prepared. I can't remember much after that… There was something but it's gone.' She puzzled about it for a moment but thinking hurt her head so much she gave up. It would come back if it was important. 'I do remember getting home and falling into bed. I think it was all rather wasted on me, poor James – I'm not used to big meals late in the evening, or so much wine…'

'Never mind, the sex wouldn't have been any fun if you were more than half-asleep,' Jenneva told her with worldly wisdom. 'Better luck next time.'

'Jenn!' Jill was shocked.

'Well, he won't just drop you, will he? Not if you had a nice time…'

'I don't know…'

'Don't know what?' Jenneva demanded. 'Look, Jill, he's the right age, he looks good, he knows how to give a girl a good time… They don't grow on trees, that kind of man, you know!'

'Yes, I know but…'

'Are you getting cold feet?'

'I suppose so…'

'It's just lack of practice,' Jenneva told her. 'You'll soon get back into the swing of it.'

'Jenn, I don't think I ever was in the swing of it!' Jill protested. 'Hugo was the only real boyfriend I ever had and we married very young. He's the only man I've ever… known more than as a friend.'

'Mmm.' Jenneva thought about it for a few moments. 'Well, maybe you need to think about it as a rather late sowing of wild oats that you didn't get around to earlier.'

'That doesn't sound like me,' Jill countered. 'I didn't sow any wild oats when I was younger, simply because I wasn't interested. There seemed to be so many more interesting things to do.' She ignored Jenneva's snort. 'And then when I was married, I was perfectly happy – so I didn't feel any need to. It wouldn't have crossed my mind. And now, well, I'm not sure that I want to now, either. Someone to take me out, drive me places, be a friendly companion – that would be good – but anything else? No, I don't think that's me at all.'

'I think you were a late starter,' Jenneva told her firmly. 'And now it's your chance to catch up. The world's your oyster, girl! You've got no strings, nothing to stop you…'

Jill sighed. It was funny how well she and Jenneva were getting on but they were worlds apart.

'You're forgetting something. I do church, remember?' Jill said. 'I actually believe all the stuff I preach on Sunday mornings – and I try to live my life to match. It's important to me – so I can't really cut loose and sow wild oats. It would feel all wrong – and for me, it would be.'

'I do despair,' Jenneva said. 'I'd give my eye-teeth for the opportunity you've got. Here I am, having to be desperately careful and only getting my fun on the odd Wednesday afternoon – and there's you with all the freedom a woman could desire – not to mention a hunky man on offer to play with! It's just not fair!'

Jill had to laugh despite herself. 'We're different, Jenn. I just couldn't do what you do. No, don't worry, I'm not going to preach at you about it! Anyway, I can't see myself "playing with James" as you put it. In fact, I rather dislike the idea that he may have been thinking of playing with me.'

'At our age, having someone to play with is worth its weight in gold,' Jenneva told her firmly. 'Keeps us young – and alive! Well, should you change your mind, I'll be happy to provide any necessary alibis, advice, anything you need. All you have to do is ask!'

'Jenn, you're wicked,' Jill remonstrated gently.

'Yes, but maybe my one saving grace is that I know it!'

When Kay rang a little later, Jill was glad to know that the emergency with their mother was over and that she was back home again.

'I really must come up and visit,' Jill said, but then she had to endure a further interrogation about her evening. Kay's final question was 'You will be seeing him again, won't you?'

'I don't know,' Jill had to admit. 'I don't think he said anything about that... not that I remember.'

Jill found it strange that everyone – well, Jenneva and Kay – seemed so keen that something more should develop from this innocent start. They seemed so sure that James would have a real interest in Jill and that it would be a good thing for her.

Was she such a sad case, Jill wondered, that she should be grateful for the attentions of the first man that came along? She had to admit that James was good-looking, very personable in fact, and charming with it. Quite a catch, in Jenn's terms. Maybe she should be flattered that he had remembered her and gone to so much trouble to provide a pleasant evening? She was genuinely grateful. Dinner at Little Barwick House had been a real treat. So when James rang later in the day, she greeted him with warmth.

'It was so kind of you to take me somewhere so nice,' she told him. 'I did enjoy the lovely dinner.'

'Well, we must do it again,' he said. 'Tell you what, have you got your diary there? I've got to get back to Birmingham today but I'll be at the Ilminster office next week. Could you manage lunch on Wednesday?'

For an instant, Jill heard Jenneva's voice saying she only got her fun 'on the odd Wednesday afternoon' and hesitated. Was that what James had in mind?

As if he had read her thoughts, he added, 'I thought I could give you lunch at that nice Italian restaurant in Langport.'

That sounded safe enough.

'I'd like that, thank you,' she told him and when she put the phone down, she felt reassured and even a little hopeful. Maybe James was offering the kind of friendship she needed. Though she remembered Eleanor's friend Liz's warning – that there were men who thought widows were sexually needy, and therefore easy. Well, Jill affirmed to herself, this one isn't.

As she went into the bedroom to put some folded laundry away, she saw the urn with Hugo's ashes on the mantelpiece.

'You don't mind?' she asked Hugo anxiously. 'It's just that I'm so lonely now. Yes, I've got a few friends – Monica, Jenneva, Eleanor – but they can't be here all the time and I'm getting bored. I'm not dead yet – and I'm not planning on doing anything wrong. You do understand, don't you?'

The silence seemed to hang heavy and she felt Hugo did not understood at all. He had been such a stickler for behaving correctly. He thoroughly disapproved of those friends whose marriages came apart because of one party or the other playing around. Guilt hit and Jill wondered whether she should ring James and back out? She was turning to go back downstairs to the phone when she remembered Sylvia Schafer and the 'love nest' in the photograph, and resentment bubbled up inside her.

'You're a fine one to talk,' she hurled her anger at the ashes in the urn. 'What right do you have to judge me, after what you've done?'

But it still all felt so wrong. She sank on to the bed, her head in her hands. How could she ever have got into such a miserable confused state? She had agreed to go out with James again – while her husband's ashes sat on her mantelpiece. Despite everything – the newspaper article, the inquest, the lot – she still found it virtually impossible to believe that Hugo had been a criminal, embezzling from the company he had loved; that he had been deceiving her, with a mistress and a love nest hidden away that she knew nothing about; and finally that he had committed suicide when it all threatened to become public.

None of it made sense.

She dragged herself through to the study. She had missed out on her morning devotions and she knew that some quiet time with God would help settle her muddled mind.

As she turned to her Bible to find the portion of scripture selected for that day's reading, some familiar words leapt out at her. The Gospel according to John, chapter 8 verse 32: 'Then you will know the truth, and the truth will set you free.'

Truth? She felt like Pilate asking 'What is truth?' Nothing about this whole mess seemed clean and truthful and believable. She felt she was floundering in a morass of unbelievable untruths.

She went back to her Bible reading but her mind was not on the words in front of her. She needed to know the truth. What could she believe? And who could she talk to? James was being kind and supportive. Maybe she could talk to him?

CHAPTER 8

✣

'Good morning, Mrs Leiston. Mr Harris wondered if you'd be free to pop in to see him later today?'

It was the receptionist from their solicitor's office. Geoffrey had warned her that sorting out Hugo's will might take a little time and that they would call her when he had got probate and cleared everything.

'No problem,' Jill replied. Her usually busy diary was as blank as if it were brand new. 'Four o'clock? Yes, I'll be there.'

As she changed out of her usual jeans and baggy sweatshirt into a smarter suit and rollneck, she remembered how supportive Geoffrey and Monica had been, driving her to the mortuary, coming to the funeral. But now the dust had settled and she was the shamed wife of a disgraced criminal, was it possible that she might have become someone a respectable country solicitor would prefer not to be too closely associated with?

She had noticed there had been no invitation to dinner, or even for coffee with Monica, but she had put that down to pressure of work. A new post as head teacher would take time to settle into. But the barb of unease had caught and she found that by half past three she was feeling nervous – and cross with herself for feeling nervous. Surely by now she was used to the sideways glances and the gossip, used to being cold-shouldered by erstwhile friends? She told herself firmly that she needed to know where she stood financially and legally, so she would just have to put on a brave face and get this interview over.

She had to admit to herself that underneath the nervousness was a solid worry. What if Hugo, in the heat of the affair with Sylvia Schafer, had changed his will in that dreadful woman's favour – and Jill was going to discover that she had been left penniless? Sternly, she reminded herself that the house had been in joint ownership so she could not lose that, and she had her teacher's pension. She would survive, however bad the news turned out to be.

Geoffrey's office was conveniently situated on the Market Square in a fine old building next to the Parish Church. Inside, a small waiting area was furnished with comfortable chairs and a low table laden with glossy county magazines. The reception desk was positioned discreetly to one side.

'Mr Harris won't be a moment,' the receptionist told her. 'Can I get you a coffee or something while you wait?'

A brandy would be more the thing, Jill found herself thinking but managed to smile and refuse politely. She was pretending to be engrossed in one of the property magazines when Geoffrey came downstairs to greet her.

She was pleased that what he offered was his usual peck on the cheek rather than a distancing formal handshake.

'Jill, my dear, it's good to see you,' he said, ushering her upstairs to his office and seating her in the chair across from his desk. 'You're a bit thinner. Are you looking after yourself properly? By the way, Monica sends her love and says when all this nonsense dies down we'll have to have you across for dinner.'

He sat back in his big desk chair and clasped his hands over his waistcoated stomach.

'Sorting out the will and everything took a bit of time, you'll understand, because of the investigation.' It was plain that Geoffrey was uncomfortable having to mention the scandal.

'Yes,' Jill responded quietly.

'Didn't seem to be much to it,' Geoffrey told her gruffly. 'Hugo's firm appeared to have all the info about what was going on and they managed to sort it all out. He managed to keep – how shall I put it? – this end completely out of it, so once the firm had checked everything to their satisfaction, I got the all-clear.'

'So there was no danger that we'd been … living on ill-gotten gains?' Jill voiced one of the horrid scenarios that had plagued her.

Geoffrey shook his head and barked a short laugh. 'Not at all. All your joint bank accounts, building society account, pension – everything – were completely above board. There was only the one dodgy bank account and all the details and documents for that were…' He paused and a further flush of embarrassment suffused his already ruddy cheeks.

'In the flat,' Jill guessed.

'Yes, that's how it was. So we don't need to worry. We can treat the will as a normal will. I assume you know that everything simply passes to you?'

Jill expelled a deep breath. The relief was enormous. 'So, despite everything, Hugo hadn't changed his will?'

'No.' Geoffrey looked perplexed at her question. 'It's the will I drew up for Hugo twenty years ago.'

'But isn't that rather strange?' Jill asked. 'I mean, if he was going to… well, let's face it, dump me, and go off with this Schafer woman, wouldn't he have changed things in her favour? And if they were going off to Spain together to start a new life, I'd have expected him to plan ahead. You know how Hugo was for seeing every detail, every eventuality was covered.'

'Well, yes,' Geoffrey agreed, though he was clearly unhappy to be discussing the matter. 'But maybe he felt honour-bound to provide for you? After all, you'd been married for how long?'

'Twenty-eight years,' Jill told him.

'Well, I don't know,' Geoffrey said. 'I didn't get any impression Hugo wanted to change anything the last time I saw him.' He stopped suddenly.

'When was that?' Jill asked curiously.

'I suppose the week before he… died. He rang and suggested we have lunch.'

'And did you?'

'Well, no. Some woman, his secretary, I suppose, rang back and cancelled it. Said Hugo wouldn't be able to make it. I thought it was a bit funny. You know what a stickler Hugo was for keeping appointments and promises! It just wasn't like him – but then I thought, maybe with all this take-over business, he was just suddenly called away or something. I know he was spending a lot of time at the Birmingham office.'

'Or the flat in Bath, the love nest,' Jill said bitterly.

'Oh, I don't know, Jill,' Geoffrey protested. 'Hugo was the last person in the world…'

'That's what I thought,' she replied with a snap in her voice.

'I'm sorry,' Geoffrey said. 'I shouldn't be talking about it and distressing you.'

Jill found herself contradicting him firmly. 'I think maybe it's healthier to talk about it than have all the gossip going on behind my back and people avoiding me because they're embarrassed and don't know what to say.'

'Yes, I can imagine. I am sorry – this is dreadful for you. I'm sure Hugo had no idea… He did seem worried, but...' Again, Geoffrey seemed to stop himself in mid-flow.

'But I thought your lunch was cancelled?' Jill queried.

'Yes, but you see, he was in the car park outside when I left that evening. He was getting out of his car just as I was about to get into mine. I was surprised to see him. He was in a tearing hurry, said things at work were worse than he'd expected and he was spending a lot of extra time trying to sort things out. I suppose with take-overs, there are always complications.'

'So why had he come to see you?' Jill asked.

Geoffrey seemed to hesitate. He shook his head. 'I can't really remember. Don't think it was anything important. Anyway, he was a bit distracted, jumpy even. I thought he was late for something.'

'Which night was this?'

'The Wednesday before he died.'

Jill thought back. 'Oh yes, I had a Parents Evening at school that night. He turned up in the middle of it. It was running late as usual. He waited in my office for me until we finished. He seemed fine then – but yes, he had been more worried and jumpy lately. I'd put it down to the take-over too.'

'Jill, we're not going to get anywhere picking over this. I know those of us who knew Hugo can't really believe what's happened, but that's how it is. We have to accept the coroner's verdict.' Geoffrey began to gather the papers together. His actions said clearly: job done.

'Do we?' Jill asked him, as something inside her stirred from the fog of confusion and disbelief into sudden anger. 'Do we really?' The question came out sharply. 'It's all right for you but this is my life that's been messed up and I still can't believe a word of any of it. You said it yourself: Hugo was the last person in the world…'

'Yes, all right, Jill. I agree,' Geoffrey said. 'But what can you do?'

'Find out the truth…'

'Ah, the truth,' Geoffrey murmured. 'Funny thing, truth.'

CHAPTER 9

✣

THE ITALIAN RESTAURANT had a small private car park tucked away at the back. Jill, spotting James's black Jaguar in one corner, parked and checked her appearance in the mirror before making her way into the restaurant.

Today's outfit, still black, consisted of a casual black velour hooded jacket and rollneck with smart black trousers. Her new hairstyle was easy to maintain and she was pleased with how she looked. She was glad, too, that much of the fuzziness in her mind seemed to be lifting, though her memory was still patchy. It was only to be expected, she had been reassured by her doctor. It would take a little time…

Wasn't that what everyone said? Time, the great healer. But Jill, a little more fiercely, was sure that truth would be the great healer – whatever it was that she discovered in the end. She simply had to find out what it was that Hugo had thought he was doing. What was missing from the inquest and everything she had been told was any reason for Hugo's totally out-of-character behaviour and Jill was determined to find out what that reason was. She was sure that James, who had been working closely with Hugo over the take-over, should have some idea of what he had been thinking and how he had been behaving those last weeks and days. James seemed to understand her need to talk about Hugo and had been kind and sympathetic.

As she entered the restaurant, James rose, smiling, and held out a chair for her. He really had such charming manners, Jill thought as she sat down opposite him. The perfect escort.

'You look wonderful,' he complimented her. 'A little thinner perhaps, but it suits you. You look even younger.'

Jill blushed with pleasure. Long unused to compliments – never Hugo's strong suit – it was delightful to be treated as a woman, even an attractive woman, again.

Jill noticed that James had a half-drunk glass of red wine by his place and wondered how long he had been there.

'I'm not late, I hope?' she asked, checking her watch.

'No. I was a little early,' James told her. 'It's nice to be with a woman who arrives on time – most unusual!'

Another compliment which raised another smile.

'What can I get you – some alcoholic Ribena?' James teased.

How pleasant it was when someone remembers what you like and what you have said, Jill thought. She found herself relaxing and smiling.

'Just the one,' she said. This time she was determined not to spoil the treat by overdoing it and punishing herself with another fierce hangover. She added, as explanation, 'I'm driving.'

'Me too,' James agreed. 'But I'm sure just one glass won't hurt.'

When the wine arrived, James toasted her, his warm brown eyes smiling at her over the rim of his glass.

'To a lovely lady!'

Jill hastily sipped her wine to cover more blushes and studied the specials menu chalked on the blackboard on the side wall. After they had ordered, James commented, 'This is a nice place. Have you been here before?'

'Yes,' Jill told him. 'Whenever I hit one of those too-tired-to-cook evenings after work, this was one of the places we used to rely on.'

'Oh, I'm sorry,' James said. 'Maybe I shouldn't have asked.'

'No, it's quite all right,' Jill assured him. 'In fact I was only saying to our solicitor the other day that it's good to be able to talk about Hugo to someone – rather than having to bottle it up because everyone's so embarrassed or scandalised!'

When the waitress had brought their food, James asked, 'Solicitor?'

'I had to go to see him because of the will,' Jill explained. 'All perfectly simple but with the embezzlement and the investigation, things needed to be checked out, and then it had to go to probate. I must admit I'd been rather worried…'

'Worried?' James queried.

'Well, I thought if Hugo was making a new life for himself with this woman, Sylvia Schafer, then he might have changed his will in her favour. I was actually rather afraid in case I'd been cut off and left without a penny.'

She shrugged and quickly drained her glass. The pain was still there inside, the bitter etching pain of betrayal and total incomprehension.

James signalled the waitress to refill Jill's glass and she gulped down another mouthful gratefully.

'But he hadn't, I hope?' James prompted her.

'No. It was still his old will leaving everything to me. It was a great relief. I mean, I've got my teacher's pension but it's not that much. Like any other wife, I was relying on my husband to have made provision for me. Old-fashioned, I know.'

'But understandable,' James smiled.

'It's about the only understandable thing in any of this,' Jill told him crossly. 'I still can't believe it. Surely I'd have known if he was having an affair? But I didn't... I didn't know anything was going on. Hugo didn't talk that much about his work. I suppose he thought all the financial stuff would be boring to me, and I expect my complaints about struggling with school budgets supported that.'

'I think the day-to-day workings of a finance department are only really interesting to the people involved,' James put in. 'But the business that it supports in this case is really interesting. We get to see such beautiful antiques, lovely paintings...'

'Yes, I'd agree,' Jill said 'but I think I was more interested in that sort of thing than Hugo. I loved going to the evening previews. I could dress up and rub shoulders with the rich, sip champagne and pretend I was choosing which things I'd bid for when I won the Lottery!'

'I'm surprised,' James told her. 'I'd have thought Hugo had an eye for the finer things in life?'

'No, not at all,' Jill told him. 'Hugo was a very plain man. He liked the quiet life, books, his garden, going for walks in the countryside, holidays in England.' She added with a sudden fierceness, 'But that's only what I thought! It turns out he wasn't like that at all. He wanted an expensive mistress and a pad in Spain, and he was willing to steal to fund it!'

Jill suddenly realised her voice had risen and the hard surfaces of the restaurant – the terracotta-tiled floor, the marble-topped tables – had sent it echoing around.

'I'm sorry,' she said with embarrassment, quickly dropping her voice. 'It's just that I find it so impossible to believe. It's so totally unlike the Hugo I knew. Look, would you mind awfully telling me what kind of person he seemed to you? You'd only have met him this past year but what impression did you get? I feel I don't know him any more…'

'No, of course, I don't mind,' James assured her. 'Let me think…'

As James began to answer, a young waitress arrived to remove their plates. Jill could not quite see what happened, but there was an instant's confusion of hands and arms and James's plate slipped momentarily out of the girl's grasp. She made a grab for it and caught it safely, but not before a dollop of rich tomato-based sauce slid onto James's pinstripe trousers.

'Oh, I'm so sorry, sir!' the girl stammered as she tried to mop up the spill, but James tore the napkin away from her.

'No, just leave it! I'll deal with it!' he barked at her.

As the girl hurried back to the kitchen with the plates, Jill heard James mutter viciously under his breath, 'Stupid bitch!'

She found herself recoiling, suddenly chilled, not just by his reaction but by the memory it had triggered.

As if a video were running through her mind, she could see herself reaching for the flashing red button on the Answermachine in James's sitting room. Worried that the message was from her sister calling on her to rush to Bath to be with her mother, she had been relieved to hear a different voice – a voice she had at first dismissed as unfamiliar but later that night had remembered as being Sylvia Schafer's. An easily recognisable, rather carefully presented husky voice. And she clearly remembered James's fury as he erupted into the room, shouting at her, calling *her* a stupid bitch.

She looked at him thoughtfully. So that was his preferred terminology for women, was it, when they did something that displeased him? Not such a nice man as she had been thinking. And what was his connection with Sylvia Schafer? Jill knew Miss Schafer was James's secretary but the voice on the Answermachine had not been the businesslike tones of a work colleague. No, those had been intimate, and confident of a friendly response. Yet Sylvia Schafer had been Hugo's mistress and surely should be mourning him, not cosying up to someone else – especially when that someone else had denied point-blank that there was anyone else in his life at that moment.

Interesting, Jill thought. It does not add up. With sudden delight, she realised her brain had clicked crisply into gear. The fog had gone. She could think clearly – and this was something she needed to think about.

Jill caught James watching her. He burst into an explanation with an apologetic smile. 'It sounds silly to make such a fuss but I've only brought the one suit and this one stains so easily! I have to stay over tonight – I've got a big meeting tomorrow morning – and I'd be in the soup if I didn't have a clean suit to wear. Finance Directors have to present the right image.'

'Yes, I know,' Jill told him drily. 'I lived with one for nearly 30 years.'

She was pleased to see that James looked a little abashed at that. Mmm, chalk one up for me, she thought.

'Shall we order dessert?' she continued smoothly. 'I'm afraid I have to meet a girlfriend at three o'clock so I need to watch the time.'

As she looked down at the menu, she wondered where that little lie had come from.

CHAPTER 10

✣

It was like a bright clear day after weeks of mist and rain. Jill's brain was alive and firing on all cylinders. It was wonderful after the confusion, misery and that muzziness that had blotted everything out. Jill knew it had been a merciful physical reaction to the shock of Hugo's death but now she was glad that her brain was back in action. She had missed its sharp incisiveness. And now she was determined to use it.

As she carefully took the long way home to support her story of seeing a girlfriend, she pondered what she should do next. Eleanor, her friend and minister, always said the way to tackle a knotty problem was to try the easiest knot first. Well, she could not really identify an easy knot. Everything seemed so neatly tied up and everyone involved appeared to be satisfied that they knew what had happened and why.

So, no untidy knots there, then, but there was one new loose thread: Sylvia Schafer. And loose was certainly the word for her if she was sharing her favours with both the past and present Finance Directors in the company! Maybe Jill could try giving that loose thread a little tug and see if the rest would unravel? After all, she did not have anything else to do. She had time on her hands, enough money thanks to Hugo's will and her own pension arrangements so she did not have to worry, and now she had a brain that had recovered its sharpness and was ready for something challenging to do.

As Jill let herself into her house, she began to plan. First she needed to find out more about Sylvia Schafer. What kind of person was she? How long had the affair with Hugo been going on? Had other people in the company noticed? Then she wanted to have a look at that flat in Bath, the 'love nest'. She was curious about it. Sometimes places had atmosphere that told you things. It was worth a try. If Hugo had been paying the rent, it might now be back on the market. It should not be too difficult to discover which letting agent was looking after it.

She took a mug of coffee into the study and switched on her computer. It only took moments to produce a long list of letting agents in Bath. She had kept the horrid tabloid article about Hugo and the love nest, cut it out and put it in what she called 'The Death File' along with Hugo's death certificate. Now she took it out again and checked the address. A scroll through the flats available in central Bath did not take long and soon she was staring at a picture of the outside of the flat.

A swift phone call produced an appointment to view.

'And you are?' the pleasant woman at the letting agency asked.

'Mrs – er…' For a moment Jill was flummoxed. If Hugo had been renting the flat, surely the agent would recognise her surname? Quickly she gave her maiden name. 'Elliott.'

'Right-oh, Mrs Elliott,' the woman replied cheerfully. 'The flat's empty so if you'd like to come to the office, you can pick up the keys from us.'

Jill put down the phone with some satisfaction at her first triumph. It felt good to be doing something about her uneasiness. Much better than sitting at home moping. She could easily combine an exploratory trip to Bath with a visit to her mother.

Next, she thought, Sylvia Schafer herself. Who could she talk to who was most likely to know about Sylvia Schafer? Who was most likely to have noticed what was going on? She thought of Hugo's PA, Penny Alford. She had been with him for years. A hard-working single Mum who had grown into a responsible job, Penny surely would have noticed any funny business. Strange, Jill thought. Apart from a condolence card, she had not heard from Penny.

Jill picked up the phone again, dialled the Ilminster office and asked for Penny.

'I'm sorry, she's not with us any more,' the telephonist replied. 'Who is that calling, please?' Jill hesitated and the voice continued quickly, 'It's Mrs Leiston, isn't it? I thought I recognised your voice. Oh, Mrs Leiston, we were all so sorry about Mr Leiston. We just couldn't believe…' There was an awkward pause then the girl continued almost in a whisper, 'Anyway, Penny was made redundant soon after. I'm sorry I don't have a number for her.'

'That's all right, Meg,' Jill said, remembering her name and grateful for her kindness. 'I'm sure I've got it somewhere.'

'You take care of yourself, now,' Meg told her. 'It must be really horrid for you. But like I said, we just didn't believe that Mr Leiston could have… Not with that Sylvia Schafer.'

Contempt and disgust travelled loud and clear down the telephone lines. 'Oops, speak of the devil! Sorry, must go now,' and the line was quickly disconnected.

Jill sat back and considered the brief conversation. So more people 'just couldn't believe' and there was no liking for 'that Sylvia Schafer'. She was glad about that. It seemed that gently tugging at the loose thread might already be producing useful information.

She searched through her address book for the home telephone number of Hugo's secretary and rang the number.

Penny sounded depressed when she replied.

'Hello, Penny. It's Jill Leiston here.'

'Mrs Leiston! Oh, Mrs Leiston, I was ever so sorry…'

'I know, Penny. We all were.' Jill cut across the condolences and continued briskly. 'Now I hear you've been made redundant. How did that happen?'

'That new Finance Director. He said he didn't need two secretaries. Well, I reckon it was *her*, that Schafer woman, who put him up to it. Anyway, Personnel called me in and said I was redundant, gave me my money and that was it. I've been trying to find something else since then but good jobs like that don't grow on trees, nor good bosses like Mr Leiston.' Penny choked on a sob. 'Oh, Mrs Leiston, I'm so sorry. I know it's worse for you…'

'Don't you worry about that,' Jill reassured her. 'Let me think: if you're not working, would you have time maybe for a bite of lunch with me? I'd enjoy that and we could talk about all this then.'

'Oh, Mrs Leiston, that would be lovely.'

'Good. Now then, would tomorrow be possible?'

'Oh yes, Mrs Leiston. I'm so bored sitting here at home.'

'Me too,' Jill told her. 'So how about Monty's Wine Bar in Taunton? There's a nice big car park right behind it. I'll meet you inside at half past twelve.'

'Half past twelve,' Penny repeated.

'Until tomorrow then.' And Jill put down the telephone, well pleased with the results of her efforts.

CHAPTER 11

※

There were several things you could be sure of at Monty's Wine Bar. One was the warm welcome from Monty, the owner, comfortably ensconced behind the bar. As he saw Jill enter, he came forward to greet her with an affectionate hug. Then, holding her by her shoulders, he put her away from him a few paces and searched her face.

'Tell me truly: how are you doing?' he asked.

'Not bad, Monty,' Jill assured him. 'It was all a terrible shock, of course…'

'Unbelievable.' Monty shook his head.

'Well, that is what I'm beginning to think,' Jill agreed. 'I was so numb at the start that I didn't take anything in. Now that I'm coming through a little bit and my head's clearer, I need to try and make sense of it. And I've got time on my hands. The school decided I could slide my sick leave into early retirement. Obviously they didn't want any scandal to touch them!'

Monty returned to his usual place behind the bar and poured out a glass of Chardonnay for her, with an acerbic comment about the Local Authority's sensitivities.

Jill accepted the wine with a smile and continued, 'I haven't anything else to do now so I decided I might as well give myself a little task, see if I can understand what happened. Then when I think I've got to the truth, no matter what that is – I realise it's not going to be nice – that's when I'll bury Hugo's ashes. I'll be able to draw a line and move on.'

'What have you done with his ashes at the moment?' Monty asked curiously.

'They're on my bedroom mantelpiece,' Jill told him with a grin. 'Nice and convenient when I want to shout at him for the mess he's left me in!'

'I never thought of you as the shouting type,' Monty told her with a smile.

'I wasn't,' Jill agreed. 'But I think I am now! Having someone die like that strips your life bare and somehow changes the way you look at the world. Your whole perspective shifts. The way you think about things changes. There's a funny, crazy kind of recklessness. So much doesn't matter any more. In fact, so little matters…'

'Mrs Leiston?'

Jill turned to discover that Penny had arrived quietly while she and Monty were talking. She greeted Penny with a quick kiss on the cheek and raised her glass of Chardonnay.

'Would you like one of these?'

'Oh, yes, please.'

'I'll bring it over,' Monty told them. 'I put you at the table beside the conservatory. It's nice and private there so you can chat away to your hearts' content.'

A little watery sunshine was penetrating into the whitewashed conservatory and reflecting into the restaurant but they were glad of the central open fire keeping the room cosy and warm.

'Oh, this is nice,' Penny said appreciatively as she looked around her. At that moment, the kitchen door swung open and Monty's wife Anne appeared. Catching sight of Jill, she came straight over to their table and gave her a quick undemonstrative hug.

'Good to see you out,' Anne told her. 'You mustn't let all this nasty gossip get you down. None of us can believe a word of it. We knew Hugo. He wasn't like that. The truth will come out, you can be sure of that.'

'Thanks, Anne,' Jill said.

Anne hurried away, leaving Jill to compose herself. She and Hugo had been regulars at the wine bar for many years and counted Monty and Anne as friends. She was touched by their loyalty. With a sudden pang, she wondered whether she had been guilty of *disloyalty*, simply accepting everything that she had been told by the police and at the inquest?

Monty brought Penny's drink, took their food order, and left them to their privacy.

'She's right,' Penny said tentatively. 'Mr Leiston wasn't someone you could believe would do anything wrong.'

Jill sipped her wine and nodded.

'And he wasn't the kind of man who played around,' Penny continued. 'You can tell the men who do. You always feel a bit grubby after one of them has been past your desk, thinking he can lean over you that little bit too close, or touch you – hand on your shoulder, that sort of thing. And the way they smile – but it doesn't mean anything … except that they think they're irresistible. And they're not!' Penny finished so fiercely that Jill had to smile.

'Well, Hugo certainly wasn't like that. But did you have someone in mind? I thought all the men at Russett & Thomson were nice?'

'Oh, they were,' Penny said darkly. 'But it's not the Russett & Thomson you and I knew any more.'

'Oh, yes,' Jill said. 'Of course – after the take-over.'

'And don't they let you know it! As if we were country bumpkins and they were the successful big city firm!'

'What do you mean?'

'Well, they couldn't do it when Mr Leiston was there. He wouldn't have stood for any nonsense. But since then, the new Finance Director and that dreadful woman have been down every Wednesday, turning everything upside down as if we didn't know what we were doing.'

'Mr Wheatley?'

Penny snorted. 'That's right. Mr High and Mighty from Birmingham, the centre of the Universe... him with his wandering hands and eyes. And that secretary of his. You'd think she owned him.'

Jill nibbled at her food. Always fresh and delicious, with vegetables from Monty's own allotment, she was aware that she was distracted and not giving it the attention it deserved. She realised that Penny was bitter at being made redundant, but she was certainly casting a new light on James Wheatley, not to mention Sylvia Schafer.

'At the inquest, and in all the newspapers, Miss Schafer said she was my husband's mistress.'

'We couldn't believe that. He wasn't the type. And she certainly wasn't his! We reckon she had her claws into Mr

Wheatley all the time.' Penny was demolishing her food with enjoyment.

Jill set her knife and fork down.

'So you don't believe she was Hugo's mistress?'

'Mrs Leiston, I'd have known,' Penny said firmly. 'I was his secretary for fifteen years. It's hard to keep secrets from your secretary.'

'So all those meetings in Birmingham?'

'The ones I knew about were genuine,' Penny said. 'They were booked into his diary by me. I took the minutes at the meetings held at this end so I knew when the next ones were, and where.'

'Maybe we should check that diary against mine,' Jill said slowly. 'I always wrote down when Hugo would be away.'

'Can't,' Penny told her. 'They said I'd lost it – but I hadn't. I wouldn't do a thing like that. I'm well-organised. You had to be in a job like mine. But it vanished and that Sylvia Schafer woman told Mr Wheatley I wasn't up to the job if I couldn't even keep track of something like a diary.'

'That is a pity.'

Penny gave a secret smile. 'I kept a copy on my organiser, though.' She reached down and ferreted through her handbag till she came up with a small electronic device. 'My Palm-Pilot. It helps me remember things. I used to check every morning at breakfast just to be sure what we were doing that day.'

'You'll miss that job, won't you?' Jill said sympathetically.

'It's not the same now – not without Mr Leiston. And Mr Russett's going to retire soon too. It's just not the same after the take-over. Not so nice at all.'

'Maybe it's for the best, then,' Jill said thoughtfully. 'Look, Penny, I wonder if you'd do me a favour? I've got my diary here. Could you bring up your diary on your organiser for… let's say August and September, and we can compare the two.'

As Penny switched on the organiser and began scrolling down to the required section, Jill became aware that the restaurant was filling up. Monty, coming through to refill their glasses, explained. 'County Court is on today so the place is full of legal beagles and their staff, and the hanging judge of course!' It was a familiar joke and Jill laughed dutifully.

She was not surprised therefore when she saw Geoffrey Harris come into the dining room with a group of similarly dark-suited men who were speaking urgently in hushed tones. He waved to her before they were shown to their table at the other side of the central fireplace.

'There,' Penny said at last. 'August and September. Let's check.'

Jill handed over her diary and watched as Penny swiftly and efficiently compared the two.

'I told you, Mrs Leiston,' Penny said finally. 'You had no need to worry. As far as I can see, Mr Leiston told you the truth about all his meetings and all the times he was away from home. Every one is in my organiser – and I booked each one, either after the meeting in Ilminster or on the basis of the Minutes from Birmingham. All above board.'

Jill retrieved her diary and popped it back into her bag. She felt a funny mixture of trembly relief and triumph. She now had one piece of solid truth: Hugo had not been lying to her about his business meetings or trips to Birmingham.

'I reckon we deserve one of Anne's wonderful puddings for that piece of detective work!' she told Penny. And as they tucked into a wicked confection of fruit and featherlight sponge and luscious cream, she began to wonder. The tangle was beginning to unravel, but she was not at all sure that she understood any better what it all meant.

It was later that afternoon as Jill was folding some clothes she had ironed that she saw the flaw in her discovery. All that she and Penny had confirmed was that Hugo had indeed had genuine business meetings on the dates he had told Jill. That did not prove he had not stayed at the flat in Bath with Sylvia Schafer on the nights when he had a late meeting or a follow-on the next day which necessitated that he stay over.

She pondered how she could check. She had never bothered to note down hotel names or phone numbers when Hugo was going to be away. There was usually just a note in her diary of the town or city where he was going and some idea of when he would be returning. Because meetings might run over and journey times were unpredictable, Hugo had always been the one to call when he got the opportunity. Jill had not felt the need to keep names and numbers. Now she wished she had. However an efficient secretary like Penny would have booked Hugo into a hotel, or if the Birmingham office had, she would certainly know where he could be reached.

Leaving the clothes in the utility room, she hurried through to the hall and phoned Penny.

'Penny, I'm sorry to bother you but I just thought of something…'

'Oh, Mrs Leiston, thank you so much for a lovely lunch. I did enjoy it.'

'I'm glad,' Jill told her sincerely. 'We must do it again now we're both footloose and fancy free!'

'I'd like that,' Penny said. 'Now what can I do for you?'

'I wondered if you had details in that clever organiser of yours of the hotels Hugo was staying at for the nights he was away?'

'Oh yes, I'm sure I do. I always booked him in. If you'll wait a moment I'll just check…'

There was a moment's pause then Penny came back to the phone. 'Oh, Mrs Leiston, I don't understand this! I'm sure I put my organiser back into my bag after we'd finished with it but it's not there now. If you'll hang on a moment, I'll just double-check.' There was the sound of a handbag's contents being tipped onto a tabletop and then serious rummaging in the contents.

'It's not there!' Penny told her in distress. 'If you don't mind, I'll just ring the restaurant and see if they've found it. It must have slipped onto the floor instead of into my bag when I was putting it away. Can I ring you back?'

Jill assured her she could and waited beside the phone till Penny rang.

'They found it?' she enquired.

'No,' Penny said. 'And they've checked for me – it's definitely not there. I don't understand this. I was sure I'd put it back. I'm ever so sorry. I don't lose things! I just don't. I'm careful about things…'

'I know, Penny.'

'I did go shopping after lunch and maybe with the wine and all, I might not have been so careful. There are a lot of petty thieves around these days. I suppose I'd better tell the police but I don't suppose I'll ever see it again.'

'Oh, I am so sorry, Penny,' Jill commiserated.

As she put the phone down, she remembered that Hugo's desk diary had gone missing from the office. Could it be that someone was trying to prevent the truth coming out? She tried to think back to the restaurant. It had got very crowded and she and Penny had been quite openly checking her diary against Penny's organiser.

But the only person she could remember in the restaurant who knew her – apart from Monty and Anne, of course – was Geoffrey. But that was ridiculous. Why would he want to stop her finding out where Hugo had been?

CHAPTER 12

※

As Jill drove up to Bath the next day, the peaceful journey through the beautiful countryside over Mendip gave her time and space to think. Recalling her meeting with Geoffrey to discuss Hugo's will, it had seemed to her that he had been rather ill at ease. She had thought at the time that it was simply embarrassment about having to mention such distasteful matters as the embezzlement and Hugo's affair with Sylvia Schafer, but there was something odd about him just happening to meet Hugo in the car park. For two such formal men, it seemed rather casual. Had it indeed been accidental? Or had there been a planned meeting? But then surely Hugo would have mentioned it to Jill and she was sure he had not. Geoffrey's final comment was strange too: 'Funny thing, truth.' Jill did not think truth was funny at all. It could be sharp and cutting – like a 'two-edged sword' as the Bible had it – or just plain and straightforward.

She considered the two men and their history. She knew that the friendship between Hugo and Geoffrey went way back, to when they had first moved to Somerset, but they had from time to time found themselves on the opposite sides of various local disputes. Hugo was invariably on the side of the underdog, the ordinary person against the developer, whereas Geoffrey, mainly because of his legal role, tended to be on the side of the big guns. And the two of them did argue vehemently about their differences and fight their opposing corners with great vigour. But they could usually laugh about it and quickly regain their normal friendship and mutual respect when the battle was over.

The latest disagreement, however, had been unusually bitter. It was over the development of the White Swan site. Once a very fine coaching inn, it was a prime opportunity for development. Hugo had supported the local council's plan to have it transformed into affordable housing in an attempt to keep young people in the town. Geoffrey had been working with the developers who wanted to turn it into a trendy shopping and entertainment centre.

'Tosh!' Jill recalled Hugo's blunt verdict. 'It just won't work round here. We're a small town and people prefer to go to Bath or Bristol for a day out shopping or going to the cinema. What we need here are more houses at a reasonable price.'

When she had asked him why Geoffrey had got so unusually irate about their differences, Hugo had sworn her to secrecy and then revealed that Geoffrey had actually invested a considerable sum of his own money in the proposals for the development.

'And he won't get it back!' Hugo had told her. 'Silly man! I could have told him it was a non-starter but would he ask my advice?'

Jill wondered if her friend Monica, Geoffrey's wife, knew that he had made such an unwise investment. Perhaps not – in which case, if that was what Hugo wanted to talk to him about, Geoffrey might feel embarrassed by her questions. To answer truthfully, he would have to admit the reason for the meeting and thus reveal the cause of their dispute. And that would mean he would risk it getting back to Monica.

Jill knew Geoffrey and Monica had gone through a bad patch in their marriage some years before – and that, Jill recalled, had been about money. She remembered that the younger Harris child had still been at school at that stage, while the elder was at university. Monica was struggling on a teacher's salary to cover tuition fees, costs of accommodation and so on for the older child, with the expectation that the burden would double the next year when the younger also went up to university.

Geoffrey had done something silly financially, Jill could not remember what, but Monica had exploded and threatened to leave, sell the house – all the usual. They had sorted it out, of course, and Jill had thought they had got over it. But if Geoffrey had made another serious mistake, if he had endangered their security in any significant way, then he was running quite a risk – and that could mean he had a reason for trying to make Jill give up finding out about Hugo's movements. Sadly, she had to admit, it made sense.

By the time she reached Bath, it was raining again. Glad to be able to park in front of her mother's house, she ran from the car through the downpour.

'Darling!' her mother greeted her with pleasure. 'Take off those horrid wet things and we'll have a coffee.' Jill knew this was by nature of a command and went dutifully to hang up her raincoat and put the kettle on.

Seated with their coffee, they burst out laughing as they saw each examining the other carefully for signs of ill health or distress.

'You first,' her mother instructed. 'How are you coping, my poor dear? It has been terrible for you.'

'Yes, Mum,' Jill agreed. 'It has been terrible but I'm beginning to come through. That horrid muzziness has got a lot less. Some days I can think quite clearly. Some days I even laugh at something – and then instantly feel guilty, because shouldn't I feel sad? So I know I'm coming through.'

'Good for you,' her mother told her. 'It does take time – and I warn you, that means years not months – but I'm glad to see you're looking much more like your old self. In fact, maybe even a little bit more like the pre-Hugo Jill.'

'What on earth do you mean?' asked Jill, taken aback.

'Well, we all loved Hugo,' her mother reassured her. 'But I always felt he kept you rather under his thumb. Living with Hugo, you became a quieter version of yourself, less bubbly, maybe even less self-confident. It happens in marriages. One partner has the upper hand and the other one goes along with it, for whatever reason.'

Jill pondered what her mother had said and nodded slowly. 'You could be right. Hugo always knew what to do and I just let him. You get to rely on someone like that. But now I have to see to everything, well, in a funny kind of way, I find I'm enjoying it – the independence, the pleasure I get from doing things right, from being able to do things.'

'Yes, I think it's easy for us women to let men – especially the old-fashioned type of man – have their way and take over.

Maybe too much? I know I did with your father, bless him. He didn't mean any harm. Probably just saw me as a helpless little woman.'

The two women laughed. The last thing Jill's mother could ever be called was a helpless little woman, but Jill did remember how her father had seemed to run everything in their lives.

'And how about you, Mum?' Jill asked. 'Are you over this latest bout?'

'Oh, I think so, but you know how it is: once you've got this horrid emphysema, it's one thing after another. A real nuisance. I just need to be a little careful. Once we get the winter over and the sunshine comes back, I'll be fine. I'm always worse in the winter.'

They talked for a while, then Jill revealed that she had another reason for being in Bath and told her mother about the appointment she had made.

'I decided I wanted to see this "love nest" Hugo was supposed to have set up,' she explained. 'It just sounded so wildly improbable, I felt I needed to see it before I could believe it.'

Her mother agreed. 'Hugo was the last man on earth you'd think would keep a secret mistress. If anything, his work and his committees were the competition in your marriage.'

'I suppose so,' Jill said thoughtfully. 'I'd never considered it like that.'

Her mother shook her head. 'I know, darling. But your sister and I did. We both thought Hugo rather took you for granted.'

'Well, he wasn't a very demonstrative man,' Jill acknowledged. 'It wasn't his way to fuss. I suppose once we were married, he didn't feel he needed to. I remember once when I was feeling a bit low, I asked him did he love me and he looked at me in total astonishment. He told me he'd married me, hadn't he? What else did I need?'

'Oh dear!' Jill's mother laughed gently. 'Silly man! I think you deserved a little bit more than that!'

'Well, that was who he was: a plain, straightforward, dependable, old-fashioned man,' Jill defended him.

'Not if the newspapers have it right,' her mother answered with a disapproving snap to her voice.

'No.' Jill sighed. 'I just can't get my head round it at all. Nobody who knew him can really believe it either. But maybe it was an aberration, a mid-life crisis.'

'He was a bit old for a mid-life crisis,' her mother told her sharply.

Jill had to laugh. 'So he was – with retirement coming up so soon. But maybe that's what it was about. He couldn't bear to admit that he was coming to the end of his working life – which meant everything to him – so he needed a little fling just to prove he wasn't finished.'

'You're making excuses for him,' Jill's mother told her crossly. 'He doesn't deserve it.'

'I don't know,' Jill said. 'I just don't know – but I'd like to. I'd really like to understand.'

She gathered up her bag and her gloves, kissed her mother fondly and as she left, said, 'And I'm jolly well going to find out!'

As she closed the door she heard her mother chuckle. 'That's my girl!'

Outside, the rain was coming down in sheets so she ducked quickly into her car, deciding that she would risk finding a suitable parking space in the centre of town. She remembered how Hugo used to tease her, 'Go on then, let's have one of your miracle parking spots.' And she'd send up a quick prayer and there, sure enough, would be the perfect space. She hoped the magic still worked.

In central Bath, the rain was running in streams down the steeply inclined streets. Finding a space close to the letting agents inevitably meant wet feet as she hopped out of the car into a puddle and then splashed against the stream to the agents' door.

'Mrs Elliott?'

For a moment Jill forgot that she had given her maiden name and looked blank, then rapidly filled the uncomfortable hiatus with, 'I'm sorry, my mind was somewhere else for a moment.'

The agent was a woman about Jill's age, more carefully coiffured and made-up but Jill supposed that was necessary for the job. She was wearing a tweedy suit with a shiny blouse that gaped a little at the buttons, but she had a pleasant smile and seemed in no hurry. She introduced herself with a firm businesslike handshake as Fran Ashford.

'I don't think we've got your details,' Fran said. 'Would you mind if I took these now?' And she gestured to a folder she had pulled from her desk drawer.

'Not at all,' Jill said faintly, wondering what other lies would have to follow to make her credible.

'Now then, we've got your name. Address?'

Without thinking, Jill gave her home address and telephone number, but the agent did not show any sign of recognition.

'And what size of property are you looking for?'

Jill hesitated while she considered her answer.

'It's just for myself, so quite small. One or two bedrooms?'

'May I ask why you're thinking of Bath?' Fran Ashford looked down at the form in her hand. 'You live in a lovely part of the world.'

'My mother lives in Bath,' Jill found herself explaining. 'I'm due to retire in spring – I'm a teacher and I live in the town where the school is – and I'd like to be near her. She's not been very well lately…'

'Oh, I am sorry to hear that.'

'I've just been to see her. She got out of hospital only last week after another little episode but she seems fine now.' Jill realised she was providing too much information but it was difficult to stop. She knew it was nervousness and tried to take a deep breath unobtrusively and slow herself down.

The agent, misunderstanding Jill's reaction, said, 'There, now, you mustn't let yourself get too upset. I'm sure she'll be fine and once you're living in the area, you'll be able to keep a better eye on her.'

Jill responded with a smile, 'Yes, you're right. I'm sure you're right.'

The woman stood up, and walked over to a small cupboard which she opened, removed a set of keys and brought them over to Jill.

'The flat is quite easy to find. It's fairly simply furnished but I'm sure you'd be able to make it more to your taste. We can talk about it when you bring the keys back.' Her smile was a clear signal that it was time for Jill to go.

'I just wondered – did the previous people have any pets?' Jill was amazed at the peculiar question she had voiced.

'Pets? No, no pets are allowed.'

'Oh good. You see I'm allergic…'

'Oh, I see. You were worrying about pet fur, that sort of thing?'

'That's right.'

'No, there's nothing like that. In fact, although it was taken as a six-month let, the people weren't there very long. In fact…' Fran flushed unbecomingly and tapped her pen on the desk.

'Yes?' Jill prompted.

'I suppose I might as well tell you,' the agent said in some embarrassment. 'I hope it won't put you off. You see, it was in all the papers. Seemingly it was used as a … "love nest" the papers called it, by some silly man who was stealing money from his company to spend on his mistress, and then killed himself when the firm caught up with him.'

'Dear me,' Jill said. 'I hope he didn't…'

'Oh no, no,' Fran Ashford hastened to assure her. 'Not at the flat. He killed himself somewhere out in the country. No, no, I assure you the flat is pristine. You wouldn't know anyone had been there.'

'Oh, good,' Jill said. 'Well, I'd better go and have a look. I don't suppose a little notoriety will do any harm. I think some of my friends might even be amused.'

'Well, I can assure you it was anything but amusing for us!' the agent snapped. 'I've no idea how the story leaked. We certainly didn't tell anybody. The first we knew about it was when the photographs appeared in the newspaper and people started talking!'

'Good heavens!' Jill murmured.

'Not the kind of publicity needed by our sort of agency, I can tell you!' Fran Ashford continued indignantly. 'How the newspaper got the photographs I do not know. We didn't let anyone have the keys. As far as I know the only person who would have had the keys was the tenant himself – and he was in no position to tell anyone! The police found his body, and I suppose he would have had the keys with him, but I shouldn't think the police would have given the keys to the press. The whole thing is very peculiar.'

'You're right,' Jill said thoughtfully as she took the proffered keys. 'That is very peculiar.'

CHAPTER 13

✣

THE FLAT WAS on the first floor of a typical Georgian house of honey-coloured Bath stone, quite near the city centre. Jill let herself in to the shared hallway, then climbed the stairs.

She could not imagine Hugo in a place like this. He liked his space and privacy, and could not understand 'people who liked to live like sardines in cities'. The detached house they lived in on the edge of Somerton had been his choice. He did not like having neighbours on either side of the wall and preferred a decent bit of garden all the way round, almost a *cordon sanitaire*. He had been delighted with the lane on one side and the little orchard that stretched back to fields where he could walk after work.

Jill hesitated as she arrived at the front door of the flat. Painted a nondescript cream, it was a perfectly plain door, with no window to see through into the flat behind. Jill fished out the set of keys from her pocket and as she inserted the Yale in the keyhole the horrid thought struck her: had Hugo used this key to let himself into the flat for his illicit assignations? A picture of Sylvia Schafer flashed through Jill's mind and she felt again the pain of betrayal, made worse by the type of woman Hugo had chosen to betray her with. How *could* he?

The thought propelled her through the door and into the flat. In the dark narrow hallway it took a few moments for her eyes to accustom themselves to the dimness. She looked around, carefully trying to take it all in. It had clearly been some time since the hallway had been decorated and the thin brown carpet was showing signs of wear. The only furniture was a plastic-framed mirror hanging above a battered hall-table.

There were three doors to the right and three to the left. First on the right was a rather Spartan bathroom, the tiles plain white and not very clean. Only a tiny window high on one wall allowed in any light. Next came a galley kitchen with a fridge, gas cooker and a selection of elderly cupboard units.

To the left was a small dining-room with a modern smoked glass-topped table and spindly chairs. A matching glass-fronted sideboard stood against one wall. The room looked out on to the street and the window rattled as traffic went past.

Next was a sitting room with an overstuffed suite in dark blue plush. There was a coffee table in front of a small gas fire and a tiny bookcase.

The back two rooms were bedrooms. On the left was a small room, almost a boxroom, into which had been crammed a single bed, a tiny chest of drawers, and a fitted wardrobe.

Jill had to steel herself before she could enter the last room. Taking a deep breath and whispering a prayer for courage, she pushed the door open and stepped inside. It was a medium-sized room with a large double bed taking up most of the space. The bed was wedged into an array of fitted wardrobes with yellow moulded fronts and tawdry brass-effect handles. A matching kidney-shaped dressing-table was placed in the window. The curtains were of a vivid floral pattern, matching the bedspread and the pleated skirt around the dressing-table.

It was all supremely awful. Jill felt an enormous wave of relief as she compared it with their light and spacious bedroom at home, decorated in palest apple-green. She and Hugo had been fortunate that their tastes agreed so well when it came to décor. They both preferred simple elegance, plain colours rather than patterns, clean lines, and good quality.

She remembered when they were first married and were looking for a sofa for their living room. They had trawled round the stores in Taunton, making each other laugh with their disparaging comments about the overstuffed, over-fancy, luridly coloured furniture they saw – so much so that Jill had to take Hugo's arm and lead him out of one shop before they were thrown out. She looked around her. How Hugo would laugh at this! He would say some pretty outrageous things too. It was just so tawdry and vulgar!

And then she remembered. This was, supposedly, the 'scene of the crime' as she thought of it. This was where he and his mistress had indulged themselves. This was what the embezzlement from Russett & Thomson was funding. This flat and this bedroom and this bed were at the heart of the betrayal that had destroyed her marriage and the future she had thought they had planned together.

She sat down on the bed to try to still the shaking and stop the tears. She would not cry, not from grief. After what he had done, he did not deserve grief. But she would let herself feel the anger that was boiling up inside.

She tried to think dispassionately: so this was it, the heart of the love nest. Well, she did not think much of it. She had been afraid the flat would be elegant and lovely, the bedroom a dream of pale colours, luxurious furniture, floaty curtains and a satin bedspread, maybe an en-suite bathroom with a bath big enough for two, a jacuzzi, marble floor – the kind of things she would have had in her dream love nest. But no. This was a rather tired, utilitarian city-centre flat for the kind of people who would use it as a dormitory and were not bothered about their surroundings.

She bounced on the bed. It was not even very comfortable. What kind of man would use this as the location for secret assignations? Certainly not Hugo. Jill had to admit that he had been rather fussy about a lot of things. And as she looked back over their life together, she realised just how much had been at Hugo's behest, to suit his prejudices, his tastes. The houses they had lived in, the style of furniture, décor, soft furnishings. She did not have anything flowery or patterned in the whole house because Hugo did not like 'fussy nonsense'. Well, she thought, now that she could, maybe she would treat herself to something fussy and feminine, just for fun. Something simple like a cushion, or maybe new bedroom curtains. There was nobody to object any more.

She stood up and flung open the wardrobes on either side of the bed, feeling the thin cheapness of the MDF doors; then she systematically worked her way through the flat, opening cupboards, checking drawers but, as the agent had said, the place was completely without any trace of previous occupation. As a last thought she checked the bathroom. There was a thin sliver of green soap on the side of the bath. She picked it up and sniffed it. It had some kind of pine fragrance.

Hugo used only Imperial Leather. Surely, Jill thought, if he had been bathing here, using a pine-scented soap, she would have noticed the unfamiliar smell when he came home?

She wandered round the flat one more time. Even if she had been thinking of moving to Bath to be closer to her mother, this flat would not be in the running. Music began to blare out from the upstairs flat and the windows rattled again as a double-decker bus trundled past. She could hear running footsteps and voices talking loudly on the stairs and she wondered how Hugo had been able to bear it. After all his protestations that he preferred somewhere quiet, why would he choose somewhere like this?

She locked the door carefully behind her and returned the keys to the letting agent.

'I'm sorry,' Jill told her. 'It's not quite what I had in mind. In fact, I must admit it's not what I'd have thought someone looking for a love nest would have chosen either. I'd prefer a bit more luxury if it was me!'

The two women laughed together.

'There are plenty of lovely hotels in Bath.' Jill was thinking aloud. 'I'd have thought somewhere like that would have been more suitable. But maybe his secretary would have heard him book it…'

'Oh, it was his secretary who came in and dealt with all the admin on the flat. Well, that's what she said she was. Then I saw her picture in the paper. It was the mistress!'

'Really?' Jill said, taken aback at this information.

'But it was all done in his name. She brought all the documentation – driving licence, bank documents and so on. We have to be so careful these days with all this terrorism and money laundering. Then she took the papers away for him to sign and brought them back the next day.'

'Really?' Jill said again, slowly, but her mind was racing. 'How fascinating. Well, thank you for letting me see the flat. I'll make sure I let you know if there's something else I'd like to view. I must get back now. Mother will be expecting me.'

As she returned to her car, she considered popping back to her mother's to make the lie true but then a tiny rebellious impulse struck. She checked how much more time she could legally stay parked and turned and headed for the shops. Something feminine, just for her. That was what she wanted. A little trophy.

Back home in Somerton, as she arranged her new lacy cushions against the bedhead and stood back to admire the effect, she told Hugo firmly, 'I reckon it's time things began to change around here. From now on, we'll be doing things my way and you needn't bother complaining about it!'

Barney the cat who had followed her upstairs stared at her as if she were mad but she was laughing as she went downstairs to put the kettle on. The telephone in the hallway rang and she stopped to answer it.

'You sound cheerful. What have you been doing with yourself?' a warm dark-chocolatey voice enquired.

'Hello, James.' Jill hid her surprise. She did not really think the familiar tone was justified. After all, she had not exactly encouraged him. She was considering a chilly response to set him at a safe distance when the thought occurred that if she wanted to find out what Hugo had been up to perhaps she should not alienate someone who might be able to help, so instead she said simply, 'I've been to Bath for the day.'

'Why?' The question was almost barked out.

Instantly on her guard, Jill chose the safe answer. 'My mother lives there,' she told him warily.

'Oh, yes, and how is she?' James purred. 'I do hope she's feeling better.'

'How kind of you to remember,' Jill replied, bemused by the way this man's moods seemed to change so quickly. 'Much better, thank you.'

'Did you have time for anything else?'

'Shopping!' Jill told him, injecting some fake feminine enthusiasm into her voice.

'Ah, you ladies! How you enjoy your shopping!'

'Yes, don't we?' Jill had to work to keep the acid from her voice in response to his patronising tone.

'In that case, maybe we could fit in some shopping for you somewhere nice? Bath again, or Bristol maybe? Yes, Bristol would be good. I could meet you and we could have lunch.'

'What a lovely idea.' Jill was thinking on her feet. Another meeting would give her a chance to probe for more information. 'Either would be good.'

'Let me give it thought,' James said.

'I think I'm free next Wednesday,' Jill offered, adding with a little laugh, 'My diary is horribly empty at the moment. It would be nice to have something to look forward to.' To add substance to the remark, she pulled her diary from her bag and riffled the pages convincingly. As she did so, the word 'Birmingham' caught her eye and triggered her memory.

'Wednesday's no good,' James interrupted her thoughts. 'I'm usually at the Ilminster office on Wednesdays. How about one Friday? I could do the Friday after next.'

Jill pretended to consider as she silently turned the pages of her diary. 'A week Friday? Yes, I think… I'm sure I could do that.'

'Excellent, excellent,' James told her as he swiftly took control of the arrangements. 'I shall look forward to that.'

Me too, thought Jill – but first there was something she needed to do. She swiftly dialled Penny's number.

'Penny, I don't suppose your organiser has turned up, has it?'

'No, Mrs Leiston…'

'Well, I've had a thought,' Jill continued. 'I'd bet Hugo liked you to book him into the same hotel every time he was staying over in Birmingham. He was such a creature of habit!'

'Yes, that's true… Even if I found a better deal somewhere else, he'd always say he preferred the hotel he knew…'

'And can you remember which one it was? I've checked back in my diary but it only says "Birmingham" each time. Hugo preferred to ring me when he got in so I never had their telephone number.' Jill held her breath as she waited for the answer.

'No problem,' Penny told her cheerfully. 'It was the Aston Towers Hotel. Sounds rather grand but in fact it's more like a family-run guesthouse…'

'Just the sort of place Hugo liked. Well done, Penny,' Jill told her delightedly. 'I think I'm going to treat myself to a trip to Birmingham so I'll just pop over to see them. A place like that, they're sure to remember whether Hugo stayed on the nights he was meant to – or sneaked off to be with his mistress!'

CHAPTER 14

It was one of those grey and drizzly and cold November Saturdays, when all you want to do is stay indoors by the fire. Jill forced herself out to the supermarket to top up her larder, then dived through a sudden squall of rain into the library.

'Jill, hi! How are you?'

Jill pulled off her rain-blinded spectacles and turned to the owner of the voice with a warm smile.

'Monica, how lovely to see you! I'm fine! How about you? Are you enjoying your new post?'

'It's taken time to adjust. Suddenly the buck stops here!'

'I know!' Jill laughed and felt sudden surprise as a wave of freedom and relief swept through her. She did not have to cope with difficult parents or governors or Ministry regulations or any of that any longer! She discovered that Monica was welcome to it all.

'I do believe you're glad to be out of it,' Monica said as she watched her friend's face crease into a relaxed smile. 'I was afraid you'd be miserable, missing it... And I've neglected you!

I'd have been in touch but I was up to my eyes, thrown in at the deep end…'

'My dear, I understand perfectly,' Jill assured her. 'And yes, of course I missed it at the beginning, but now I feel really free …'

'Look, we can't chat here,' Monica said. 'We're blocking the production line. Shall we get our books, then have a coffee? We can catch up properly then.'

They quickly returned their books and headed to the fiction shelves for replenishment. Jill was amused to see that Monica read romances. She herself always and only read crime novels. Not the gory kind, or too psychologically nasty – they gave her nightmares. No, she liked a nice puzzle where she could pit her wits against the criminal and try to get the answer before the fictional sleuth.

Clutching her finds to her chest, she followed Monica to the check-out then they hurried together in the rain across the square to the tearoom. The windows were misted up but once inside, they were glad to see there was a spare table left.

Coffee and blueberry muffins ordered, they settled down to the serious business of catching up. Jill was delighted that Monica was so obviously enjoying her new responsibilities.

'You were ready for it,' Jill told her. 'You had been a deputy long enough.'

'I was beginning to feel that if I didn't get a headship soon, I'd be too old and would have to retire without ever having achieved it,' Monica admitted.

'Well, I'm glad it's worked out. I'm perfectly happy you're doing my job. It's good to know the school is in safe hands.'

'Are you sure you're not bored and miserable?' Monica prodded.

'No. In fact – this may sound a bit daft – I'm having fun.' Jill lowered her voice and confided, 'I'm doing a bit of sleuthing.'

'You're what?' Monica was astounded. 'What about?'

'Well, Hugo's death and all that stuff about embezzling and the mistress and everything. It just wasn't the man I knew,' Jill explained. 'I felt I couldn't really draw a line underneath it all and move on until I could really understand what had been going on.'

'Gosh!' Monica gulped.

'Once I began to come out of the shock – it does completely knock you over, you know – there were so many things that just didn't ring true. I've always been nosy, so I thought, well, I've got time on my hands so I might as well use it. And now I'm discovering there are more questions than answers, and to be honest, somehow that's fun. It challenges me, gives me a kind of purpose, I suppose.'

'I think that's awfully brave of you,' Monica told her. 'I think I tend to bury my head in the sand, hoping things will blow over.' She hesitated, then plunged on, 'For example with this silly development project at the White Swan. You did know Hugo told Geoffrey in no uncertain terms that he was being an idiot investing in it? Of course, Geoffrey hadn't told me anything about it. He knows I'm extra-thrifty money-wise especially compared with him, and he knew I'd disapprove. So when he and Hugo had a barney about it, Geoffrey was terrified I'd hear about it and find out what he'd done. Which of course I did. Somerton's a small town after all and you can't have a stand-up row with your best friend without everybody knowing.'

'Yes, I had heard,' Jill said carefully.

'Silly man,' Monica continued affectionately. 'I know he does some crazy things occasionally, so I make sure I have a little nest-egg tucked away to cover any disaster. Then when he comes home and confesses the latest daft scheme he's put money into and lost, I can be calm and unworried. Well, Hugo didn't know this and seemingly he was concerned that Geoffrey would get in too deep and really mess up our finances so he had a right old go at him!'

'Oh dear, that does sound like Hugo!' Jill said ruefully.

'He told Geoffrey he had no right to jeopardise my future!' Monica laughed. 'Real white knight stuff! Gave Geoffrey a lecture on charity beginning at home, pointing out it was a betrayal of my trust in him…'

'Yet, all the time he was betraying my trust with that dreadful floozy.' Jill found she had spoken her thoughts out loud.

Monica stopped in her tracks and stared at Jill. She shook her head. 'That can't be right. Hugo wasn't a hypocrite,' she said. 'A pain sometimes, when he was so sure he was right and everyone else was wrong. But he was never a hypocrite.'

'Yes,' Jill agreed. 'That's certainly what I thought.'

Clearly uncomfortable, Monica rushed on. 'They made it up, of course.'

'Who? Geoffrey and Hugo?'

'Yes. I could see how unhappy Geoffrey was so I told him I knew and wasn't cross. I suggested he pull out what he could of our money and then make it up with Hugo. So when Hugo rang the next day to fix lunch, Geoffrey was delighted. Of course, then Hugo's secretary rang and cancelled it but he did pop round after work. He was waiting in the car park for Geoffrey and Geoffrey told him what he'd done. They shook hands and were just about to go for a drink together when Geoffrey says Hugo got very jumpy. Seemingly there was a car circling the Market Square and every time it went past, Hugo got more and more twitchy. He dived off in a hurry and that was the last time Geoffrey saw him.'

'Mmm,' Jill said, considering what she had been told. 'Well, I'm glad they made it up. They always used to after one of their disagreements – hot and loud, but always short-lived. Men are funny! I didn't know about the car, though. I wonder where that fits in. Does Geoffrey have any idea what kind of car it was?'

'I didn't ask, but I will, if you like.'

'Yes, I think I would.'

'You *are* sleuthing, aren't you?' Monica commented.

'Yes, I think I am.'

Monica finished her coffee. 'I must run.' She paused and kissed Jill's cheek. 'Good luck with the sleuthing. You're right. It is all a bit funny when you start to think about it.'

Back home, with the cat purring on her knee, and her library books piled up on a small table beside her chair, Jill was feeling restless. She did not want to read, but she could not go out. The rain was now constant and the sky was dark.

She dislodged Barney, made herself a mug of coffee and carried it upstairs. Maybe she should sort Hugo's clothes and get them ready to go to the charity shop. That would give her something to do. It seemed so final though. Half-heartedly, she pulled open the wardrobe door. There in front of her was Hugo's favourite checked shirt. The one that had appeared in the photograph of the Bath flat.

As she stroked its soft worn fabric, she remembered the letting agent's puzzlement about how the press had got into the flat to take the photograph and her insistence that they had not supplied the keys. Jill turned back to the bed and opened the drawer of the bedside table on Hugo's side of the bed. There was his key-ring with its familiar cluster of keys. She had removed the keys to the office and his company car and returned those to the firm in the week after his death. She ran the rest of the keys through her fingers, checking them off: their house front door, back door, garage door, shed padlock, a duplicate to Jill's car key. Pretty much what she had on her own key-ring. She went back downstairs for her handbag and pulled out her keys to check. They were identical.

So where were the keys to the flat in Bath? Had the police removed them? But wouldn't they have returned them to Jill with the other keys, as Hugo's property? Anyway, she thought, how would anyone know which were the keys to the Bath flat amongst a bunch of unidentified keys? That was another of Hugo's *bêtes noires*: people who labelled their keys and then were surprised when they were burgled or had their cars stolen. 'Idiots, asking for trouble' was what Hugo used to say – so of course his keys, and Jill's, were never labelled.

Jill rummaged around the drawer in Hugo's bedside table but found no further keys. She worked her way through jacket pockets and trouser pockets in his wardrobe. No keys. Downstairs in the study, she searched every drawer in Hugo's desk. Again, she drew a blank.

So where were his keys to the flat?

CHAPTER 15

SATURDAY'S RAINY WEATHER had given way to a bitterly cold and windy Sunday. At church, the shock and scandal over Hugo's death had given way to sympathetic support, though Jill still found it difficult to cope with being asked how she was, as if she had been ill. What do you say? Say you're fine, grin, and horrify the people who want to see you as a sorrowing widow? Do the brave-face-covering-the-broken-heart bit and be told firmly you need to pull yourself together and get on with your life? You could not win. So she just smiled politely and murmured meaningless noises, trying not to pull away from the questioner too abruptly.

The service itself was a blessed respite where all she had to do was stand up and sit down with everyone else, follow the readings and the hymns, and relax in the glorious stillness of prayers and sermon. It was balm to her soul.

Eleanor was leading worship and afterwards, instead of the formal handshake at the door, Jill was moved when she was engulfed in a warm hug. She had not realised how much she missed physical contact and for a moment felt a pang of real anguish – no more hugs, no more love… Maybe Jenneva had a point. Maybe she should take advantage of her freedom and find someone who would give her those hugs…

When she got home there was a message from Monica.

'I need a break this afternoon,' she announced. 'Do you fancy coming with me for a walk along the front at Lyme Regis? It will blow the cobwebs away.'

Jill rang back and agreed enthusiastically. It was exactly what she needed to take her mind off the sudden loneliness that threatened to overwhelm her. She threw together a scratch lunch then went to change into warm cord trousers and a thick sweater. She was engrossed in the Sunday supplements when the doorbell rang. Monica stood outside.

'Get your walking shoes on, girl, and we'll hit the hills.'

'I thought we were doing Lyme?'

'We are. It just sounds better.'

At Lyme Regis, they were fortunate to get one of the last parking spaces in the car park at the bottom of the hill. Getting out of the car, the wind blew through Jill's hair and whipped sudden colour into her cheeks.

'Told you we needed this,' Monica said.

In perfect harmony, they set off along the promenade and walked in companionable silence to the Cobb where stormy waves were throwing sheets of water over the top. Dodging the showers of water, the two women fought the wind to get to the end of the Cobb and huddled together, looking out over the wild waves and the view of the Dorset coast.

'I love it here,' Jill announced. 'I could never move.'

'Good,' Monica told her. 'I was worried you might want to get as far away as you could.'

'I felt like that at the start,' Jill admitted. 'All those sideways glances in the shops and the whispering when everything hit the newspapers. It was awful. But now, well, I suppose I'm so angry about it all I won't let the gossip drive me out.'

'Good for you,' Monica said and linking her arm in Jill's, she fought their way back along the Cobb and to the tearoom at the end of the promenade.

'Whew!'

'But worth it!'

'Absolutely! I haven't felt this alive for ages.' Jill peeled off her jacket, hat and gloves and settled into the comfortable chair. When they had ordered tea and toasted teacakes, they sat back and grinned at one another.

'Good one!'

'Crazy coming out in this weather.'

'Yes, but…'

'Well, if we can't be crazy at our age…'

'Two respectable head teachers!'

'Come on, Monica, you mustn't let Geoffrey's legal respectability grind you down.'

'Look who's talking! I always thought Hugo kept you in check.' Monica's hand flew to her mouth. 'Oh, I shouldn't have said that. I'm so sorry!'

'No, you're right. Hugo would never have done something daft like dodging waves on the Cobb – but I love it. I loved him too, but maybe, yes, life with him was a bit quiet for me. If anyone was going to kick over the traces and have an affair, it should have been me!'

Monica's mouth dropped open. 'Good heavens! I never thought to hear you say that.'

'Good old, respectable, quiet-living, church-going…'

'Lay-preaching, example-setting…'

'Oh, how boring!' Jill laughed at the staid picture they were conjuring up. 'Was I really?'

Monica nodded. 'Well, only to people who didn't really know you. Your real friends…'

'The Female Mafia as Hugo called them.'

'That's us! We knew who you were really, and we knew that lots was being kept under the surface. I suppose now…'

'Yes,' Jill agreed. 'Now I can be truly me. Sad, isn't it, that I couldn't be me when Hugo was alive? I was perfectly happy – well, maybe not perfectly. But happy enough.'

'I sometimes wonder how happy is happy enough? There have been a few rough times with Geoffrey. He worries me with his cavalier attitude to money. He loves a little flutter – only it's not on the horses, it's always some ridiculous development project any fool can see isn't going to work.'

The tea arrived and they warmed their hands gratefully on their cups. Then their toasted teacakes were set before them, shining with melted butter and requiring serious attention.

'Mmmm, that was wonderful!' Jill said, wiping the lingering crumbs and butter from her mouth.

'Totally scrumptious,' Monica agreed. She looked at her watch. 'Better get back. If I'm not home in time for *Time Team*, Geoffrey will start worrying – he knows I love it.'

'Me too.'

'I suppose it's another kind of detecting, so it'd be right up your street,' Monica suggested.

'I hadn't thought of that, but yes, I suppose so.'

As they drove back, Monica asked, 'Have you made any more progress on the sleuthing?'

'Well, there is something rather peculiar,' Jill said and she told Monica about the missing keys and the letting agent's puzzlement about how the press had got into the flat to take the photograph.

'You could always ask the newspaper,' Monica suggested. 'Say that as you're now responsible, you need to get the keys back to the letting agent. See what they say. They should have given them back to whoever gave the keys to them.'

Jill gazed at her friend in admiration. 'I hadn't thought of that. What a clever idea. I'll do that first thing tomorrow.'

Dropping Jill at her house, Monica kissed her goodbye, then as a thought occurred to her, she apologised. 'I forgot to ask Geoffrey what kind of car it was that was circling Somerton Market Square the night Hugo was there. I'll try to remember and ask him.'

'All pieces of the jigsaw puzzle,' Jill said with a smile. 'And I wonder what kind of a picture they're going to produce?'

CHAPTER 16

✣

On Monday morning, Jill woke feeling bright and cheerful. The walk in the storm-fresh air of Lyme Regis had invigorated her and she was eager to get started. But first, she needed to sort out her thoughts. She had told Monica there seemed to be more questions than answers and currently they were all jumbled together in her mind. As an inveterate list-maker, what she needed was a notebook and a pen – and a list.

After feeding Barney and having her own breakfast, she took herself through to the study and settled down at her desk. As every day, she drew her Bible and books towards her. For many years, it had been her custom each morning to read a small portion of the Old Testament and a small portion of the New Testament, with a modern commentary to help her understand and meditate on the reading.

So often in the past, she had found direct help and guidance from her daily reading. She remembered with a smile the day one of her staff at school had mentioned her unease about life after death. She had been fretting that her father might be stuck for all eternity with the horrid second wife he had married after the tragic death of his much-loved young wife who had been her mother. Just that morning, Jill had been reading the very passage in the gospel of Luke where Jesus taught on that subject. They had both found a lot of comfort from the 'coincidence'.

So she opened her Bible with quiet anticipation, but as she read the Old Testament passage for that day, her eyes widened:

'…justice is driven back, and righteousness stands at a distance;

truth has stumbled in the streets, honesty cannot enter.

Truth is nowhere to be found, and whoever shuns evil becomes a prey.

The Lord looked and was displeased that there was no justice.

He saw that there was no-one to intervene.'

Although the words came from so long ago (Isaiah 59:14-16a), they seemed like a direct challenge. Jill felt suddenly ashamed that she had simply accepted what she had been told, that she had not intervened to make sure that what was said was the truth about Hugo's death, and that justice was indeed done.

She sat very still, trying to calm her racing thoughts. Was this speaking to her – or was she reading too much into the passage?

She turned hesitantly to the New Testament and paged through to the portion for the day. As she read, a familiar verse leapt out at her:

'Then you will know the truth, and the truth will set you free.' (John 8:32)

Well, truth was certainly what she wanted – and she did feel that once she knew the truth, she would be able to draw a line under the whole terrible experience and move on, which probably meant the same as being set free. At the moment she felt in limbo, caught in a web of 'facts' she found hard to believe. That did not feel like freedom.

She pondered quietly. Coincidence? Or not? What was needed was clarity. She put her Bible and commentaries back in the desk drawer, then pulled out a notebook. Chewing the end of her pen for a few moments, she tried to order her thoughts, then she began to list all the things that puzzled her.

First, the embezzlement: she didn't know how much money was involved or exactly what Hugo had done. She did not even know how long it had been going on for. So, how could she find out? The only source she could think of was James Wheatley. In his position as Finance Director, and as the person who had carried out the investigation into the embezzlement on the firm's behalf, he was surely the best informed and would be able to explain to her what it all meant and what had happened.

Next, the love nest and the missing keys. Who had given the press access to the flat? Did the photographer still have the keys? She noted down Monica's clever idea: phone the newspaper and ask.

Third, Hugo's business trips away from home. Penny had assured her that they were legitimate, but Hugo could have combined a legitimate business trip with an assignation with his mistress. Jill would check that one next week with the people at the Birmingham hotel where Hugo was supposed to have stayed.

Jill paused and read through her list, then she added Penny's organiser: did she really lose it or was it stolen? It seemed rather too much of a coincidence, especially after Hugo's desk diary went missing. Could she ask Geoffrey if he had noticed anything at the wine bar that day, anyone lurking near them or paying them particular attention?

Finally, the car circling the Market Square the night Hugo met Geoffrey: whose car was it? Monica had promised to ask Geoffrey. It might mean something but Jill could not imagine what.

She sighed. Each disconnected point was like such a tiny piece of a jigsaw puzzle. None of it seemed to make sense. She reminded herself that she had decided to simply try pulling at the loose ends to see what came of it. It was clear that there were still plenty to pull.

Getting out the ring binder she had designated the Death File, she removed the tabloid cutting, checked the name of the newspaper, then pulled the telephone towards her and dialled directory enquiries.

Put through to the news desk of the tabloid, she had her words prepared.

'Oh, I am sorry,' the girl at the other end said when she heard Jill's story.

'Please don't worry It's just that now I've got all the clearing up to do and I need to get the keys of the flat back to the letting agents so we can terminate the lease…'

'Oh right, I understand. I'm afraid I don't know offhand which of our photographers it was that took the picture. Can you remember whether there was a name on the side of the pic?'

Jill pulled the cutting towards her and examined it carefully. 'No, there's no name.'

'That's strange. We always credit the photographer. How about the name of the writer of the story?'

Jill read out the byline: 'Edward George.'

'Oh good, Ed's here. I'm sure he'll be able to explain everything. Let me transfer you.'

And in a moment, Jill was explaining her search for the keys to a chap with a friendly northern accent.

'Call me Ed,' he told her. 'I'm sorry I can't you help you with the keys. We didn't have the photographs taken by one of our people on that occasion. It was a tip-off, you see. We just got sent the photographs in an envelope through the post, with a typed note about your late husband's tragic death and the date of the inquest. It seemed a good story so we checked it out…'

Jill held on to her fury with some difficulty. A good story indeed!

'How did you check it out?' she asked with icy calm.

'Well, *cherchez la femme*, don't you know?' Ed appeared oblivious to the offence he was giving.

'The lady?' Jill repeated with an effort to keep him talking.

'Miss Schafer… Well, she pretends she's a lady, but I'd say she's not.'

Jill ignored this tempting titbit and focused on her quest. 'How did you know to talk to her?'

'We had her photograph, didn't we, and we had her name and where she worked, so it was easy,' the journalist explained confidently.

'Didn't she mind?' Jill asked.

'No, I don't think so,' Ed told her. 'She didn't seem surprised either. She was actually very cooperative. People can be about the funniest things. You wouldn't believe...'

Before he could launch into reminiscences, Jill cut across with the quick question, 'So the envelope you got contained her photograph as well as the picture of the flat?'

'That's right. It's not unusual for us to get a collection like that. When someone wants a bit of publicity, they often tip us off that way.'

'Publicity?' Jill echoed, horror tinging her voice.

'Oh, people have lots of reasons, sometimes very strange reasons, for wanting publicity about things,' Ed told her. 'Revenge often enough, even if they'll come out of it badly. Money. Sometimes people think they can *sell* a story...'

'Did Miss Schafer ask for money?' Jill asked sharply.

'Oh, no. We asked her if she wanted to sell her story, but she said she'd told us enough.'

'You can say that again,' Jill breathed.

'Look, I'm sorry I can't help you...'

'Oh, but you have,' Jill told him and she thanked him before putting the phone down and looking at it with amazement. Pulling loose ends was producing unexpected results. Could it have been Sylvia Schafer who had sent the photographs to the tabloid? But what reason could she have had? Surely it could only damage her own reputation and her position in the firm? Not that it seemed to have. She was still James's secretary and appeared to be throwing her weight around in the Ilminster office and making herself very unpopular. And it certainly was not for the money. Ed had said they had offered her money for telling her story and she had refused. So was it revenge, then? But revenge against whom?

Hugo was dead by that point in the whole sorry saga. It did not make sense.

Jill tried to calm her whirling mind and sort out what she had learnt. Someone had tipped the newspaper off about Hugo and Sylvia Schafer and the Bath flat, and about the embezzlement from Russett & Thomson. Now, who could possibly want publicity for such a story?

It only took a moment to be connected once again to Ed George.

'I'm sorry to bother you again,' Jill began. 'I just wondered, did you check the story about my husband embezzling from Russett & Thomson with anyone actually in the firm?'

'Oh yes, my dear,' Ed answered readily. 'We spoke to the Finance Director there…'

'But Hugo was Finance Director,' Jill interrupted him.

'No, no, the other one.'

'The other one?' It took a moment before the penny dropped. 'James Wheatley, at the Birmingham office?'

'That's right. He confirmed everything, so we ran with the story.'

'I see,' Jill said slowly. So first Sylvia Schafer had cooperated with the press, then James Wheatley. But surely the breaking news would damage the firm's reputation? On the other hand, maybe it would all have got out anyway so it was thought better to get the story straight first time round, to scotch any rumours or misinformation that would do even worse damage.

She wondered what Jim Russett, the Managing Director, had thought about it. He would have had to be told of the press interest and how it was being handled. She knew he hated the press with a vengeance after the story they ran about a fake Monet the firm had unwittingly handled a few years back. It had left Russett & Thomson and its advisers looking very silly. The local press had had a field day with it.

'Mrs Leiston,' Ed George interrupted her thoughts. 'Would you like to tell me why you are asking these questions? Oh, I understand about the keys to the flat, but it seems to me there's more of a story here than I realised.'

'You're right,' Jill confessed. It was a relief to come clean. 'But I don't have any answers for you. I'm just trying to piece it all together. I find it all so hard to believe and I need to get it clear in my mind. There seem to be such a lot of loose ends…'

'I think I've told you everything I know,' Ed assured her. 'Is there anything I could do to help you?'

Jill thought about it. There was one person who kept cropping up in the loose ends department and that was Sylvia Schafer, but Jill could hardly go and talk to her. Wronged widow approaching mistress? No, Jill could not face that. But maybe Ed could?

'How would you feel about approaching Miss Schafer again?' Jill suggested tentatively. 'She's the person I'd most like to get some answers from. She seems to be right in the middle of all this. But I'm sure you see I can hardly talk to her myself!'

'Mmm.' Ed considered it. 'Running a follow-up, that sort of angle? Anything in particular you'd like to know?'

'Everything!' Jill told him emphatically. 'How the affair began, what attracted her to him and vice-versa, how serious they both were, what difference it makes to her now…'

'Well, that certainly is the sort of thing we'd want to know for a follow-up. You'd make a great journalist, you know! Tell you what, I'll give her a ring and see if she'll play ball. Maybe

I should run up to Birmingham and meet her. I could do with a day out, even in this weather!'

'I'm planning to be in Birmingham next Wednesday,' Jill said. 'I thought I'd check out the hotel where Hugo used to stay – or was supposed to be staying. I'd like to find out what they can remember – whether he was in the habit of sneaking off at night for assignations with that woman.'

'How about we meet up for a drink afterwards and compare notes?' Ed suggested.

'That would be good,' and Jill agreed to meet Ed at a coffee bar in the New Street Station complex where they could chat before catching their respective trains. Maybe they could pull together some of those loose ends.

CHAPTER 17

A CALL FROM her sister Kay later in the week had Jill packing a bag and hurrying over to Bath to give their mother some company and support. The latest attack had not been severe enough for her to need hospitalisation again but she did need someone to be with her until she was completely recovered. Kay had a wedding in Cumbria to attend so Jill was needed to help out.

By Friday afternoon, Jill's mother was well recovered and cheerful again.

'Why don't you take yourself out, darling?' she suggested. 'I'll be all right. In fact, I think I'll have my afternoon nap as usual. You'll be quite bored if you stay in. Go and hit the shops!'

Jill laughed. Her mother was certainly sounding more like her old self.

'I'll do that – and maybe have tea somewhere with naughty cream cakes!'

But even as she wandered into interesting shops, Jill found her mind kept circling round the loose ends. She wondered would Ed George be able to find out more from Sylvia Schafer? Would she have the courage to ask James to explain about the embezzlement when she saw him in Bristol next Friday?

She realised she had stopped in front of a small boutique next door to the letting agents who had dealt with the 'love nest' flat. Lying about who she was had sat uneasily on her conscience. She checked to see if Fran Ashford, the agent she had spoken to last time, was in. She was, and there was no one else there. On impulse, Jill pushed open the door and approached the woman with a smile.

'Hello, again,' Jill said. 'I wonder, do you have a moment?'

'Yes, indeed.' The woman looked up and seemed pleased to have company. 'It's nice to see you again. How can I help you?'

Before she could lose courage, Jill plunged ahead.

'The thing is I didn't tell you everything last time I saw you. My mother does live in Bath, and she has been ill. In fact, I'm staying with her at the moment. But, my real name is Jill Leiston. I gave you my maiden name. You see, my husband was Hugo Leiston, the man who was supposed to have rented the flat I went to see. I just couldn't settle. I had to see it… to get some idea… I thought maybe you wouldn't let me just go and look at it if I wasn't a proper punter… so I made up the story. I'm sorry, but…'

Fran Ashford listened to her with wide eyes.

'Golly, yes, I do see,' she said finally. 'Yes, I do indeed. I think, if it was me, I'd have wanted to see the flat too. Look, would you like a cup of tea? I was just going to have one.'

'That's very kind of you…'

'Not at all. Then we can talk more comfortably.'

Fran went away and returned shortly with a tray with cups and saucers, milk and sugar, and a plate of biscuits. Placing the tray between them, she settled herself back behind the desk.

'Now, is there any other way I can help you? It must have been terrible for you. If you want to look at the flat again, you just have to say.'

'No, I don't think so. But I did wonder. You never got Hugo's keys back, did you?'

'The tenant's set? No.'

'You see, I checked, at home. I haven't got round to giving his clothes and stuff away, yet. I know I'll have to get round to it soon. Anyway, I had a good look and there definitely aren't any extra keys among his things,' Jill explained.

'That is most strange. Since we spoke, I've been puzzling about how the photographer got in. Somebody must have given the keys to the press.'

Jill reached for her cup of tea and drank gratefully.

'I wondered too,' she said 'so I spoke to the newspaper. It turns out that it wasn't one of their photographers who took the pictures. It seems that they were sent an envelope with the two photographs in it – the one of the flat and the one of that woman – plus notes on what it was all about. They checked out the information and when they got confirmation, they ran the story.'

The letting agent took a long swallow of her tea and reached for a biscuit. She munched it, looking thoughtful.

'How peculiar,' she said. 'So who would have taken the photograph of the flat? Obviously someone who had access.'

'That's as far as I've got,' Jill admitted.

'Well, it couldn't have been your husband,' the agent stated flatly. 'He was dead by then, poor man. So who's left?'

The two women looked at each other.

'Are you thinking what I'm thinking?' Fran asked.

'The only person left who might have had access to the flat was the mistress,' Jill said slowly.

Fran nodded. 'That's right. The woman who came in and dealt with the paperwork. And collected the keys.'

They sipped their tea in silence as they thought through the implications.

'You couldn't ring her and ask for the keys back, could you?' Jill suggested.

'That's worth a try. At least that way we'd find out if she's got them.' Fran nodded again, as if making up her mind. 'Good idea. Let me just grab the file for the telephone number. I'll do it right away while you're here.'

Jill drank the rest of her tea while Fran went to the filing cabinet and extracted a bulky file. Setting it down on her desk, she opened it and turned to a letter which Jill recognised had been typed on Russett & Thomson letterhead.

'Right!' Fran said. 'Let's see what happens.' She punched the number into the phone and as she waited, she pushed the file towards Jill. 'Have a look at the contract while I'm talking. It's all properly signed, sealed, etcetera, believe me.'

Jill drew the file towards her but at that point Fran began to talk in a gushingly friendly voice.

'Miss Schafer, I'm oh so glad to catch you. This is Fran Ashford from Clariford Letting Agents in Bath. We met a few months ago....'

Fran stopped, clearly interrupted by Sylvia Schafer. She continued with some apparent difficulty.

'No, no, Miss Schafer… All I wanted… I wondered if… if you had the keys for the flat we arranged for Mr Leiston. We didn't get them back, you see.'

Her face went still as she listened intently. Jill flipped over the pages of the file till she came to the contract. While she waited, she read the terms and had just reached the last page when Fran finished her conversation with Sylvia Schafer.

'I perfectly understand, Miss Schafer. Yes, of course. Say no more about it. Thank you for your time.'

She put the phone down and sat back in her chair. Jill dragged her gaze from the file and paid attention.

'She says – Miss Sylvia Schafer – that her handbag, with the keys in it, was stolen. She reckons someone who wanted to make trouble for your husband must have taken the keys and got the photographs. She said her photograph was already in the flat, framed – and then whoever did it sold the story to the newspapers.'

Fran leaned forward. 'What do you think about that?'

'That is very strange,' Jill said. 'The newspaper man didn't say they were asked for money for the package with the photographs in it. It's possible, I suppose… though there do seem to be a lot of things rather conveniently going missing. But I do know one thing,' she added, her voice shaking as she pushed the file towards Fran. She stabbed a finger at the contract. 'That isn't my husband's signature.'

CHAPTER 18

✣

'It's an attempt at Hugo's signature,' Jill explained. 'But it's not his. He was left-handed and his handwriting was frankly appalling! I always said his signature looked like a spider who'd got into the ink and was trying to crawl uphill!'

'You're quite sure?' Fran Ashford asked.

Jill nodded. 'I'm totally sure. I'd know Hugo's signature anywhere. It was very distinctive and although this is a good try, it isn't quite right.'

'Mmm, I suppose it would have been easy enough for someone else to sign the paperwork,' Fran said. 'After all, Miss Schafer took the papers away and brought them back the next day. We simply assumed that the papers had been completed and signed by your husband, and that it was his cheque for the deposit and the first month's rent. After all, all the signatures looked the same.'

Jill considered carefully.

'Can you remember,' she asked, 'did you get any identification for Hugo?'

Fran flipped back through the file. 'Yes. We took a copy of his driving licence. Here it is. I'm afraid my partner took everything at face value. She decided that there was no hurry doing the credit or bank checks because your husband had a reputable job – and of course there was a cheque for the deposit and first month's rent.'

'Can I have a copy of the driving licence?' Jill asked. 'You see, again, I'd say that's not Hugo's signature. In fact, well, I thought Hugo still had one of those old-fashioned paper licences like mine and this is one of those new ones with the photo on. The police gave me all the things Hugo had on him when he was found so if his licence was among them, I'm sure to have it. I'd like to compare this with the licence I've got at home, just to be sure.'

Fran swiftly made a photocopy and gave it to Jill who put it carefully in her handbag.

As she rose to leave, Jill paused. 'You wouldn't happen to remember which bank the cheque came from?'

'It will be in the file. We note down all those sorts of details, just in case, you know…' She flipped through the file and stopped at a form headed BANK DETAILS.

'Yes, here we are: Nat West, and it's a Birmingham address. I can give you a copy. You probably should have a copy of the lease too…' As the photocopier whirred softly, Fran continued. 'Everything happened so quickly that we didn't get round to checking details…'

Moments later, Jill was leaving the office feeling well pleased with her impulse. She now had copies of the lease, what had been provided as Hugo's driving licence, and details of the bank account from which the rent for the flat had been paid. She would check the last two the moment she got home.

One comfort was the knowledge that the flat had been leased so very recently, only a couple of weeks before Hugo's death. If Hugo had been having an affair with Sylvia Schafer, it had not long reached the stage where it required a rented love nest.

Back at her mother's house, Jill was delighted to find her awake and bright and cheerful.

'I've been doing more snooping,' Jill told her.

'Oh, darling, please do be careful! If there is anything fishy to find out, there may be people who don't want you to know.'

'I'm pretty sure of that,' Jill agreed. 'And I will be careful. Anyway, I'm making sure enough people are aware of what I'm up to so if I suddenly disappear off the face of the earth, someone will put two and two together…'

Kay came back from the wedding in Cumbria with a fine array of photographs to share with their mother so Jill took her leave on Saturday and set off home. She was just about to empty her overnight bag when a thought struck her. Plan A had been to simply pop up to Birmingham on the train on Wednesday, visit the hotel where Hugo always used to stay and get the information she needed, then, with James safely out of the way at the Ilminster office, pop in to the auction rooms and have a little snoop before she met up with Ed George at Birmingham New Street Station to compare notes before taking the train home again. But now she wanted to visit the Nat West branch with the Birmingham address where Hugo had allegedly opened the account to hold the proceeds of his embezzlement and pay the rent on the love nest. Jill had a number of questions for the bank manager there. Clearly she would need more time than she had originally planned.

She ran downstairs and telephoned the Aston Towers Hotel.

'I wondered if you could fit me in on Tuesday evening? I know it's short notice but my husband always stayed with you…'

Jill listened to a torrent of regrets and sympathy and was rewarded with an assured booking.

'We'll be so happy to see you. I'm glad you felt you could come to us. We were so sorry…'

It warmed her heart that so many of the people who had known Hugo were sorry or disbelieving. She went back upstairs and faced the urn on the bedroom mantelpiece.

'I don't know if we're getting anywhere,' she told Hugo. 'But I'm going to go on till I find out.'

She turned and emptied out the drawer of Hugo's bedside table on to the bed and sorted through the contents: keys, a selection of cufflinks, his soluble indigestion tablets, nail clippers and nail file – all the paraphernalia he kept there. And there was his wallet. Jill had gone through it out of curiosity when she had brought Hugo's effects home from the mortuary, but she had been so numb nothing had really registered. Now she sat down on the bed, murmured an apology to Hugo for what felt like prying, and proceeded to examine the contents carefully.

She removed Hugo's debit card on their joint account, his two credit cards: one he used only for business, the other a joint card on their building society account, his National Trust life membership card, English Heritage card, a few other familiar membership cards – and each one with that easily recognisable signature. Tucked inside the wallet where she had replaced it was the little folded newspaper clipping of local market days. And finally his driving licence. As she had thought, it was the older type, a folded sheet of paper, without photograph but with signature.

She reached for her handbag and pulled out the photocopies Fran had given her. The driving licence was obviously one of the new kind, with a tiny photograph. Jill studied it carefully. It certainly looked like Hugo. Next she pulled out the copy of the lease document. She flattened out Hugo's licence and compared the signature on it with the signatures on the lease and on the other driving licence. They were quite close, but not quite right. Because Hugo was left-handed he wrote at a slightly sloping angle, and this showed especially in his signature – probably very difficult for someone who was not left-handed to copy.

She turned and gazed at the urn.

'I'm sorry, my love,' she told Hugo, as tears began to gather. 'I did doubt you and I'm so sorry.' She brandished the two photocopies. 'Somebody set this thing up. This isn't your driving licence, and these aren't your signatures.' She choked back a sob. 'I used to be so horrid about your handwriting! Crabbed, cramped, and always going uphill! Well, now I'm glad! Oh, Hugo, how I miss you!'

Flinging herself on the bed, she wept till the terrible pain subsided once more. Disturbed by the noise, Barney appeared from downstairs and nudged her.

'This won't do,' Jill told him and roughly dried her eyes. 'I need to tell someone what I've found out.' It was definitely not Hugo's licence so that was something tangible to start with.

'That photo though,' Jill wondered aloud. 'Where would someone get a couple of matching passport-type photos of you?' As she gazed at the urn, imagining Hugo there in the life, she suddenly remembered. When Russett & Thomson had taken over the Birmingham firm, all of the senior staff had had their photographs taken for press releases.

'Mug shots,' Hugo had told her. 'We look like a bunch of criminals, rather than respectable businessmen!'

For someone inside the firm, it would be easy to get hold of the unused prints – or was everything digital these days? Would that have been even easier?

'I'll find out,' she told Hugo firmly. 'Just you wait and see.' She patted Barney and urged him down off the bed, then she tidied Hugo's wallet, minus the driving licence, and all the bits and pieces back into the drawer and popped it back into place in the bedside table. 'This comes with me – and maybe then goes somewhere safe.'

As she followed Barney downstairs, she pondered where would be safest. The bank? No. Their wills and the house deeds were kept at their solicitor's. Geoffrey! That's who she should tell. She was reaching for the telephone when it rang.

'Geoffrey! You must be psychic! I was just thinking of you!'

'Monica was badgering me about what kind of car was circling Somerton Market Square the night I saw Hugo. I promised for the sake of peace I'd ring you. I don't know if it means anything…'

'Tell me, Geoffrey. At this stage, I need all the information I can get – and then I've got something important to tell you.'

'That's funny. That's what Hugo was saying… Anyway, it was a black Range Rover. You know one of those big 4x4s. Rather smart, actually.'

Jill sat down slowly. A black Range Rover. She could not think of anyone she knew who drove one of those. Jenneva Rawlings had a maroon one, though you usually could barely see the colour for mud.

'Geoffrey, I think I'd better come round to see you at the office. Could you spare me half an hour on Monday afternoon? I have quite a lot to tell you and I need you to look after something for me.'

CHAPTER 19

※

JILL WAS TIDYING up the house before leaving to see Geoffrey late on Monday afternoon when Fran rang her.

'I don't know if this is connected in any way with what you're working on,' Fran started.

'Fran, what's the matter?' Jill demanded. 'You sound shaky.'

'I am. We've had a break-in,' Fran said, adding in explanation, 'We usually shut on a Monday but I'd left something in the office, so I popped in this afternoon and discovered the break-in.'

'Good heavens,' Jill exclaimed. 'How unpleasant. What was taken?'

'Well, that's the strangest thing. Nothing as far as I can see. We only keep petty cash in the office and that hasn't been touched. There aren't any keys missing. But the back door had been forced so we know someone's been here.'

'How strange,' Jill replied, her memory darting back to the peculiar break-in they had experienced a couple of weeks before Hugo died. Then, too, it had seemed that nothing had been stolen but suddenly Jill began to wonder. She remembered Hugo asking later that week where his favourite shirt was – and then it had appeared in the photograph of the flat in Bath, along with a few other odds and ends. Excitement tingled in her veins and a sudden presentiment flashed into her mind.

'Fran, would you just check that file we were looking at the other day. Just on the off-chance. See if anything's missing from it.'

There was a pause and Jill could hear Fran moving across the room, opening the filing cabinet, then the thump of the file on the desk, and Fran picked up the phone again.

'Right. I've got it…' Her voice faded away, then returned loudly. 'Well I never! You're right, Jill. The lease document isn't there, nor the photocopies of the driving licence and the cheque. Well! Wasn't it a good job I gave you copies of those. Without them, you'd never have known there was anything wrong with those signatures.'

'Which is exactly what someone is trying to achieve,' Jill said thoughtfully. 'Well, I'm off to my solicitor now with those very copies for him to put in his safe.'

'Should I tell the police about this?' Fran asked. 'They came round a little while ago but at that point I didn't think anything was missing so they simply sympathised and went away.'

'I'll talk to my solicitor about it. I'm sure he'll have some ideas about what we should do.'

And Geoffrey did.

'Leave it alone, Jill,' he told her bluntly. 'It won't bring Hugo back. Even if what you're saying is right, you don't know what kind of person is behind all this and you could be putting yourself into serious danger.'

'But Geoffrey,' Jill protested. 'I've got some real evidence: the licence, the false signature on it and the lease, …'

'I can see that,' he assured her. 'And I'll keep those documents safely here. I do agree with you that it's very odd but it's up to the police to sort this out, not you dabbling on your own. I'll have a word with someone I know. I'm sure if they feel there's something to follow up, they will.'

Jill sat back in her chair and stared at him. 'Hugo was your friend,' she reminded him as steadily as she could. 'Don't you want to see his name cleared? Don't you want to help me?'

'Yes, of course. But it won't do any good. It won't make any difference to the facts.' Geoffrey was clearly trying to soothe. In a softer voice, he continued, 'Hugo is gone, my dear. What's past is past. It's time to let go.'

It was like a red rag to a bull. Jill exploded out of her chair. Fists on Geoffrey's desk, she confronted him, 'That may be your opinion but it's not mine. I don't believe Hugo did any of those things he's been accused of. I think he was set up and then…'

'And then?' Geoffrey asked.

'And then killed,' Jill said flatly. 'I think they got rid of him.'

'Whoever *they* are.'

'That's right. Whoever *they* are,' she said defiantly. 'And I want to find out who they are and I want them brought to justice. I want Hugo's name cleared…'

'And your own,' Geoffrey inserted.

Jill stared at him in outrage.

'What are you saying? That I'm only interested in retrieving my reputation?'

'It might be thought…'

'Well, it's not true. I'm doing this for Hugo. And if you won't help, I'll jolly well do it myself!' and with that she flung out of Geoffrey's office.

Thinking about it next day as she sat in the train to Birmingham, she considered she might have chosen a slightly less schoolgirlish turn of phrase. Poor old Geoffrey! He was such a cautious soul – except of course where his little investments were concerned. She valued her friendship with Monica and thought they had managed to sort out between them what it was that had made Geoffrey seem a potential suspect.

Still, he had been the only person she had recognised at Monty's Wine Bar the day Penny's organiser was stolen. Was it wise, then, to take the photocopies to him? She reassured herself that he had not reacted in any way that suggested recognition or guilt. He had been 100 per cent professional, a bit fuddy-duddy in fact. Maybe he was just trying to calm her down, gently turn her aside from her quest to stop her getting any false hopes. Well, it was not going to work. She would go on until she knew who was behind it all, and why. Then, if Geoffrey had indeed talked to someone he knew in the police, it would be time to bring them in.

By the time she reached Birmingham, Jill was quite tired. The train had been surprisingly crowded and she had to admit she was not used to busy commuter trains. Her taxi turned in to the shingle car park at the front of the Aston Towers Hotel and she got out and looked around. It was a large Victorian house with double bay windows and a huge front door standing invitingly open. Jill paid the taxi driver, then grabbing her overnight case she hurried into the hotel as rain began to fall.

Inside, a welcoming hallway was decorated in warm shades of gold and cream and a smiling young woman of Asian origin stood behind the reception desk.

'Hello. I'm Jill Leiston.'

The girl came round from behind the desk and took Jill's hand in a warm handshake, relieving her of her overnight case at the same time.

'Mrs Leiston, we are delighted to have you here. Now, I've put you in the room your husband always had but if you would prefer another room…'

'No, no! That would be lovely.'

'We thought it would make you feel close to him. These things are important.'

Jill smiled at the girl. 'Thank you. It is so kind of you to understand.'

'Mr Leiston, your husband, was such a welcome guest. He was almost one of the family. We understand there was some nonsense in the papers about him but they must have just made it up. You know what those tabloid papers are like! We knew him. It just wasn't true.' The girl dismissed it all airily and led Jill up the wide curving staircase. 'I'll show you the room.'

Delighted with the girl's straightforward approach, Jill allowed herself to be led into a pleasant bedroom. As she looked around, she recognised that this was indeed to Hugo's taste: comfortable in a quiet understated way, the colours muted and toning, no patterns, and simplicity of line in the furniture. Even the en-suite bathroom was plainly elegant and Jill could imagine Hugo setting out his shaving things on the shelf above the washbasin.

'Yes,' she murmured to herself. 'This is just right.' And the sharp contrast with the ugly florid flat in Bath reassured her. Hugo had not rented it. It had never been a love nest with that dreadful woman… So why had Sylvia Schafer said it was? She hoped Ed George would be able to prise that information out of her tomorrow. Meanwhile, Jill had things of her own to check out.

CHAPTER 20

❀

By the time, Jill left the hotel next morning, she was feeling cherished and reassured. Not only had the Patel family checked the hotel register and been able to confirm unequivocally that Hugo had indeed stayed with them on all the occasions he had been away from home at take-over meetings, but the lively family were able to add corroborating evidence in the way of little stories linked to their lives.

'I remember that time,' the eldest son told her, pointing to an early booking. 'I was feeling a bit down 'cos I'd done badly in my exams.' He was studying accountancy at Birmingham University. 'I was even thinking of packing in Uni, getting a job like my friends, even just helping out here. But Mr Leiston told me I'd regret it. He encouraged me to stick with it. He even took time that evening to go over some of the stuff I didn't understand... He was brilliant. The next time he was here, he asked in particular how I was getting on and it was great to be able to tell him I'd passed the resit!'

'That time,' the younger daughter pointed at another entry in the register, 'I'd had the interview for my place at Cambridge. When I got home I just tore in to tell everyone that it had gone well and Mr Leiston was there in reception, chatting to Dad after supper, and he laughed and said of course I'd done well and he ordered a bottle of champagne so we could all celebrate.'

Everyone seemed to have a story to tell. Jill smiled. It was so like Hugo to get involved with this very likeable family. Not having any children of their own, he always took an interest in young people and tried to help them wherever he could. And this family had repaid that interest with fierce loyalty. Not one of them had believed the newspaper report, dismissing it as fantasy tabloid journalism. They had been shocked to know Hugo was indeed dead and simply could not understand what could have driven him to suicide.

'I wouldn't have said he was that kind of person, Mrs Leiston,' Mr Patel senior told her. 'He was always so well-balanced in temperament. A calm man, and a kindly one. It's very strange. When I last saw him – that was late on the Saturday afternoon – he apologised that he was leaving a day early. He said he'd done everything he could here and he would be glad to get home.'

'The Saturday?' Jill queried. 'I was expecting him home on the *Sunday* afternoon.'

'That's right. He was booked in for Saturday night but, as I said, he left early,' Mr Patel said.

'He seemed disappointed,' the accountancy student son commented. 'I was out on the drive trying to fix my motorbike and I saw him putting his bag in the car.'

'Did he say anything?' Jill asked.

'No. I waved and called goodbye but just at that moment his mobile rang and he turned away to answer it. He drove off immediately afterwards.' The boy shrugged. 'I'm sorry. I've no idea what was said.'

'Thank you,' Jill said thoughtfully. So Hugo had planned to come home on the Saturday. Then he had had a call on his mobile. Was it possible to check calls? Maybe they could find out who had rung him. But then she wondered: where was Hugo's mobile? She did not think she had seen it amongst the items returned to her by the police. That was puzzling.

Another thought struck her: surely if he had had his mobile with him, he would have called her to say he was on his way home early? That was strange, and very unlike him.

Jill took an affectionate farewell of the Patel family, thanking them warmly for their help, then directed her taxi to take her to Solihull, to the Nat West branch whose address was on the cheque that had paid for the flat in Bath. After a few moments, she was led into the manager's office. She had phoned and set up a meeting with him. First though she had to endure the usual condolences before she could get down to business.

'I'm tidying up all the loose ends,' Jill explained.

'Yes, of course.' The bank manager steepled his fingers and waited.

'I wondered, since I haven't been able to find a statement on this account, would it be possible for me to have an update?'

The bank manager quickly accessed the account on his computer screen, printed out a statement and handed it over to Jill. It was very short. It started with the opening of the account only two weeks before Hugo's death. The amount that had been deposited, by cheque, to open it was exactly the amount required to cover the cheque for the deposit and the first month's rent for the Bath flat. No further deposits had been made, nor withdrawals. The account was completely empty.

'Nothing there, I'm afraid,' the bank manager said.

'No,' Jill said slowly. 'Is that why no statement has been issued?'

'Oh, we sent out a statement,' the man assured her. He checked his screen. 'On the twenty-first of the month as usual.'

'But I wasn't able to find it in any of my husband's files.'

'Maybe he destroyed it. People often do.'

'Not Hugo,' Jill said firmly. 'He was a Finance Director by profession and scrupulous about paperwork. He kept everything like that.' A thought occurred to her and she asked, 'Where did you send it? To our home address in Somerton in Somerset, or did you send it to the office address in Ilminster?'

Again the manager checked the screen and this time read out a completely unfamiliar Birmingham address.

'I'm sorry,' Jill apologised while she scrabbled in her bag for pen and notebook. 'Could you repeat that?' As he did, she wrote down the address and stared at it. Then she shook her head. 'That address means absolutely nothing to me.'

Another mystery, she thought. Something else to investigate. And that reminded her of the last thing on her list of questions for the bank manager.

'I wonder, would it be possible to see the document my husband signed to open the account?'

The bank manager did look a little surprised but a swift phone call to the front office brought in a smart young man with a thin file. The bank manager opened the file and removed a form.

'Here it is.'

It was strangely reassuring, Jill thought, even familiar and welcome to see this not-quite-Hugo's signature once again.

She smiled and stood up, offering her hand. 'Thank you very much. You've been very helpful.'

Outside she managed to flag down a taxi and showed the driver the address she had copied down.

'I'm afraid I have no idea where it is. I don't know Birmingham at all,' Jill said.

'It's in Edgbaston, ducks,' the driver told her. 'No problem. Hop in.'

So she climbed in and enjoyed a pleasant drive through suburban streets before she found herself set down outside an Edwardian house with a neatly tended garden. It was obviously a large family home. There was a double garage to one side and the house and surroundings gave every sign of prosperous living. But what could she do now?

A postman was approaching so she stood on the path leading up to the door and began fumbling in her bag.

'Drat! Where is that key?' she muttered loudly as he approached.

'Lost your key, love?' he asked her.

'It's in here somewhere. My friend gave me a key so I could let myself in. It'll be at the bottom here.'

The postman laughed. 'Women's handbags! Everything but the kitchen sink in those things!' He offered her the letters he was carrying. 'You have these. I'll be getting on.'

Jill continued rummaging till the postman turned the corner and was out of sight, then she turned the top letter over.

It was addressed to Mr and Mrs James Wheatley. As she gasped, a woman appeared round the side of the house. Tall and elegant with fair hair beautifully cut in a flattering bob, she was wearing slimline jeans and a bright pink sweatshirt under a green Barbour jacket, with a chunky leather bag thrown over one shoulder. She caught sight of Jill and smiled.

'Hello. Can I help you?'

'I'm so sorry,' Jill said. 'I was passing and stopped to check if I'd brought my mother's house keys with me – she prefers I let myself in, she's so deaf! – and I think the postman must have thought I lived here and he gave me your post.' She handed the bundle of letters over.

The woman glanced at the name and address on the top one and smiled again. 'Yes, these are ours,' she said. 'He was probably saving himself coming up the drive!'

Jill forced herself to smile back. 'Well, I must be on my way then. I need to get back to New Street Station.'

'Can I give you a lift?' the woman asked. She stuffed the letters in her bag and pulled the garage door open. Jill's eyes narrowed as she saw the vehicle inside.

'New Street is on my way,' the woman was saying. 'You'll find it impossible to get a taxi around here.'

'That would be a great help,' Jill said, trying to marshal her thoughts. 'I really don't know my way around Birmingham. I was visiting a friend and decided to come by train rather than car.'

'Trains can be much more convenient and less tiring. By the way, I'm Emma Wheatley.' She held out a hand.

Jill, feeling rather guilty, took it. 'And I'm Jillian Elliott,' she said, remembering it was probably wiser not to give her real name.

A few moments later they were on their way. Emma chatted away cheerfully as she negotiated the suburban streets and then the busy city-centre roads.

'Edgbaston seems rather nice,' Jill commented.

'Oh yes, there are some very nice parts of Birmingham. I wasn't at all convinced when James – that's my husband – got a job here but I've decided I quite like it. There are good schools for the girls…'

'Oh, lucky you,' Jill exclaimed. 'How many children do you have?'

'Just the two and they're at the monsters from outer space stage at the moment. The clothes they want to wear! The music they listen to, if you can call it that! I'm sure we weren't like that. And of course, their father absolutely adores them and spoils them rotten. Daddy's girls who can twist him round their little finger. Mind you, he's such an old softie almost anyone could!' Emma laughed happily and neatly manoeuvred the big car up to the entrance to New Street Station.

'Thank you so much for the lift,' Jill told her. 'I'd have got completely lost and would never have found a taxi!'

'No problem,' Emma said again. 'It's nice to have company.' And with a smile and a wave she was gone.

Jill was thoughtful as she made her way into the station. So James was not at all the footloose, fancy free, separated man he had told her but instead was the proud father of two teenage girls and husband to a charming pretty wife. And the vehicle Emma Wheatley had been driving was a black Range Rover.

CHAPTER 21

It was a funny combination – this grimness as she thought about James and the lies he had told her, and the genuine relish she was feeling as the pieces of the puzzle began to take on some kind of shape. Jill found she was smiling to herself as she deposited her overnight case in a locker at the station, then took herself back outside into the chill Midlands air to find a taxi.

'Aston Antiques Sales, the antiques auction house,' she told the driver and settled back into the seat to watch the city streets go by.

'Going to an auction there, miss?' the driver enquired.

'That's right,' Jill told him.

'After anything in particular?' he asked.

'Just a browse – for fun!' she replied and felt the now-familiar surge of pleasure. It would be fun too, slipping into the auction with no-one knowing who she was, having a chance to snoop around and get a feel for the place. Maybe she would find out something more to help her.

'Good luck!' the driver said, startling her out of her thoughts. But then she laughed, remembering he thought she was simply going to an auction, and thanked him, with a silent prayer not for luck but for guidance.

Within a short while, they had arrived at a complex of converted warehouses beside a canal.

'How pretty,' Jill exclaimed. On the other side of the canal, the combination of smart paintwork on the restored buildings and a waterside pub with tables and chairs set outside even on a wintry day made the area seem almost continental.

'It's quite different from how it was,' the driver told her. 'There's been a lot of money put in and now it's very popular round here – and expensive! You'd hardly believe it but not so long ago it was pretty much derelict. Not an area for a lady like yourself to come to.'

'That's hard to imagine now,' Jill said, as she climbed out of the car and paid the driver.

'Hope you get what you want!' the driver called as he waved goodbye.

Me too, Jill thought. She paused and took time to gaze around her. The auction house was located in an old warehouse, fronted by a large car park, its concrete surface rough and potholed. It looked as if it needed still more investment to bring it up to the standard of the area around it.

A bit shabby, the building itself could have done with a coat of paint. The sign above the big double doors was new, reflecting the take-over, but the place was smaller than Jill had expected and much more run-down. In comparison the Ilminster set-up covered a huge area with storage warehouses, offices for the valuers and the administration staff, as well as the auction rooms themselves, two for less valuable items, and the other for fine art and antiques. She was surprised but maybe for a successful country firm, buying a smaller city-based auction house made perfect business sense. She could not quite see how.

Around her was the bustle of cars arriving and people streaming into the building. Jill joined them and found herself in a small reception area with a desk arrangement like a small bar across one corner. Behind it, a man and a woman were arguing while a queue formed, waiting for their attention.

'Well, you'll just have to. Jenny isn't here today,' the man said sharply.

'Somebody could have warned me!' the woman protested. 'I'd have worn flat shoes.'

They pushed their way past the queue and left, still arguing. A young blonde girl behind the counter smiled apologetically.

'Can I help anyone?'

Jill picked up a catalogue – a photocopied typescript stapled in the corner, not like the glossy catalogues with photographs that Russett & Thomson produced for their sales.

'Do you have a bid number?' the girl asked. 'Or would you like one now?'

Jill hesitated. At Ilminster, you needed to produce proof of identity before you got a bid card – all the money laundering precautions were securely in place, Hugo had seen to that – but she did not want to reveal who she was.

'It won't take a minute,' the girl assured her cheerfully. 'Just write your name and address down here and I'll do it in a jiff.' No request for proof of any sort, Jill noted. She complied and soon was the proud bearer of a laminated card with a bid number in the name of Jillian Elliott.

She looked around her with interest as she followed the flow of people into the auction room. It was not at all what she had expected. The room was simply a big plain warehouse space. The walls were a dirty cream and the goods for sale were piled on trestle tables lined up against the walls, although there was one staffed table with some glass cabinets protecting the more precious items. Jill could not help comparing this spartan, even grubby set-up with the rich wine-coloured walls of the Fine Art and Antiques auction room in Ilminster. It was carpeted and well lit, and the décor enhanced the furniture and the porcelain and silver that was for sale.

Jill followed the browsers round the room, noting the poor quality of the china and glassware on the tables. There was a selection of moth-eaten stuffed animals and birds in ancient cases, some fishing tackle and other sporting kit which she passed hurriedly. Surely there was something of interest? She stopped for a moment in a quiet corner and flipped through the list. The entry for some silver napkin rings caught her eye, and further down the list were some assorted gentlemen's cufflinks. Hugo had loved cufflinks and she had always sought out interesting antique ones to give him for his birthday and at Christmas.

The silver was probably in the glass cases so she meandered her way in that direction, pausing occasionally to examine an item on a table as if she were a genuine browser. She found she had to stand on tiptoe to see some of the things in the glass case and one of the staff, the woman she had seen downstairs complaining about not being warned to wear flat shoes, noticed she was having some difficulty, and asked if she could bring anything down for her to see.

Jill pointed to the silver napkin rings and when they were set on the glass table top, she turned them over and tried to look knowledgeable about hallmarks. She let the flow of the woman's quite well-informed commentary wash over her.

'They're very nice,' she said, handing them back.

'Anything else you'd like to see?' the woman inquired as she put the napkin rings back on their shelf.

Jill consulted her catalogue and pointed to the number. 'Silver cufflinks?' she asked.

'Ah, yes,' the woman said. 'We've got some rather nice ones.' She reached under the counter and brought out a small cardboard box. She opened the box and began placing the contents on the counter, sorting the cufflinks into pairs.

Jill tried to show some interest though the first few pairs were cheap and modern. But then the woman turned over a heavier silver pair with a distinctive art nouveau motif and Jill had to stifle a gasp. Her fingers were trembling as she reached over and touched the cufflinks.

'Nice, aren't they?' the woman commented. 'Best of the lot, I'd say, though these are nice too.' She rummaged in the box and brought out another pair, heavy plain silver with bevelled edges. 'There's a little bit of damage…'

Jill stood rigidly looking at the two pairs of cufflinks. They were Hugo's, she was sure of that. She had given him the art nouveau set for his birthday in August and he had worn them frequently since then, declaring they were his favourites. The plain silver pair had been another gift, an anniversary present many years before, and he had worn them often, enjoying the heaviness and simplicity of the design, until he had accidentally caught and damaged one of them. They had been in the drawer of his bedside table awaiting repair.

Jill pulled herself together with an effort.

'Yes, they are,' she said. 'Very nice. Thank you for showing them to me.' She tried to move away casually but her mind was racing. How had two pairs of Hugo's cufflinks got into this sale?

Jill sank gratefully into a chair and tried to calm herself as the auction began. She was fiercely determined she would get those cufflinks back even if she had to blow her cover and bid for them herself.

CHAPTER 22

※

Gradually the chairs around Jill filled up. She noticed many of the men were in scruffy anoraks and muffled in scarves. A couple of them were in shabby tweed jackets and thin flannels. A group of women in loud nylon parkas with voices to match and flashy costume jewellery were leaning against the wall to her right and bantering with the staff. Studying the assembling buyers gave her a few moments to collect her thoughts.

Finding the cufflinks had been a shock – but so too was the discovery that James had a wife and two adoring daughters, not to mention the fact that the address given for the Nat West bank account had been James's home. Tugging at loose ends was dislodging some very disconcerting information.

To keep her mind calm and focused, Jill listened carefully to the bidding and marked the final hammer price on her catalogue. It was remarkable how little each item seemed to sell for. Many of the porters shouted in with commission bids and at times it got quite confusing who was doing what. One item produced some telephone bids fielded by two obviously 'office' members of staff – one a man in a suit, the other a young blonde girl in a dangerously short miniskirt and skintight sweater.

The staff maintained a rolling production line with one porter in an apron – the only one in any kind of uniform – holding up the item currently for sale, then when it was sold, passing it on to the next member of staff in the line behind the long table who passed it on till it was finally back where it had come from. It seemed a slick and effective system.

The noise of chatter from the open door of the café behind the saleroom was distracting and Jill had to force herself to concentrate till the lot with the cufflinks came up. An old hand at bidding at auction, she was surprised at how difficult it was to gain the auctioneer's attention. He seemed to have fixed ideas about who would be permitted to bid. Jill in desperation finally waved her hand with its bid card strongly in the air and called out, to ensure he knew she was there and determined to bid.

The only other bidder was a large lady on a specially cushioned chair at the front. Obviously a regular, probably a dealer, Jill thought, she looked very put out at Jill intruding on her patch. But Jill was determined. She kept bidding. There was no way she was going to let Hugo's favourite cufflinks go to anyone but herself.

The hammer crashed down finally and Jill sat back with relief. She could feel her heart pounding as though she had been running. Done it. Now at least the cufflinks would be back where they belonged.

'Jill?' a voice said in her ear.

She jumped in shock. No one knew she was here. But there at her shoulder was James Wheatley, leaning over her.

Frantically she checked her memory. Yes it was Wednesday, so what was he doing in Birmingham? Hadn't he said he always went to Ilminster on a Wednesday?

'What are you doing here?' she found herself demanding.

'I could ask you the same thing,' he replied. 'Come on.' He pulled back her chair. 'We can't talk here.'

She considered rapidly. There really was nothing she could do without making a scene and she did not want to do that. Maybe there was some way she could turn this to her advantage.

She managed a smile and allowed herself to be helped from her chair. (As if I were some ancient crone, she thought crossly). She followed James from the auction room and out into the corridor, where he turned towards her. He had been frowning but now a smile lit his face and he greeted her with a welcoming beam.

'What a lovely surprise! You should have said you were coming and I'd have arranged to meet you and show you around…'

As he spoke, he bent to kiss her cheek and she had to steel herself not to flinch away as the memory of James's pretty blonde wife, Emma, flashed into her mind. He had certainly lied to her about that – and she was beginning to think there was much more he had lied about. Once trust was gone, it was gone and she no longer trusted this man.

'Oh, it was just a crazy impulse,' she told him airily. 'Last minute thing. I was feeling restless and I couldn't settle… I was thinking about Hugo and I suddenly realised the one place I hadn't visited with him was the Birmingham office and I thought I'd like to.' She waved her hands helplessly, trying to give the impression of the helpless, aimless widow. 'I don't know. I just thought maybe it would help settle me, so I jumped on the train and here I am! The auction was going on when I arrived and I love auctions…'

'See anything you fancy?'

'Not really,' Jill said. 'I got some jewellery I liked the look of. I'll need to make sure I pay and collect it.'

James nodded, apparently accepting her comments at face value. 'Did you have any plans for the rest of the day?' he asked.

Jill's mind raced. How far could she push her luck? Ah well, nothing ventured…

'Well, while I'm here,' she smiled winningly 'is there any chance of that guided tour? Though I'm sure you must be busy…'

James consulted his watch. 'Not at all. Let me show you around now and then we can pop out for a bite of lunch.'

'Thank you, James. That would be lovely.' Jill schooled her breathing back to normal. She would have to be calm to handle this.

'You've seen the main auction room,' he said. 'We have another larger one for the poorer quality stuff on the other side. It's not quite as grand as the Ilminster set-up.'

'But it works,' Jill responded politely.

'Yes,' James said absently. 'It may not look much but it works. For example, I saw you on the cctv. I was just having a quick look and I couldn't believe my eyes! I had to come in and make sure. You really should have let me know you were coming!' And for a moment there was a flash of – was that anger in James's eyes?

Jill felt like a naughty schoolgirl as James led the way up the stairs that led to the office area. The stairs were rather dreary as though the offices were an even poorer relation. And on arrival at the office floor, it was clear that was indeed the case. Compared with the offices of Russett & Thomson in Ilminster, Jill was surprised at how few staff seemed to be around. She reckoned that most of them were doubling as portering staff for the auction that day, like the woman who had been complaining she had not been warned to wear flat shoes. It reinforced Jill's sense of how small an enterprise it seemed to be. Perhaps they had been in need of rescue from the take-over?

'Basically, Hugo shared my office when he came to Birmingham,' James told her, showing her through a small outer office into a larger corner room with views of the canal. A large desk with a computer on it stood underneath the window and James perched on the desk.

'Your secretary isn't around?' Jill asked casually.

'Early lunchtime today. She's meeting someone,' he said dismissively. 'Now, unless there's anything else you'd like to see, we can go downstairs and sort out your purchase, then nip out for some lunch.'

'I'm glad to have had a chance to see the building,' Jill said as she looked around James's office. 'I couldn't get a picture of it in my mind so it was like a missing jigsaw-puzzle piece in Hugo's life. Thank you for showing me around. It really helps me fit everything together.'

For a moment, Jill thought James looked alarmed so she smiled at him and said, 'I know it's silly, but when you've lived with someone for close on thirty years, I suppose you think you know them. I can picture Hugo in the Ilminster office but of course the take-over was fairly recent so I hadn't had a chance to get a picture of him here. It felt like a hole in the picture. Now I've been here, that's good. It's funny how these little things seem to matter.'

'I suppose so,' James said slowly. 'I must say you seem to be coping rather well.'

'I've got good friends,' Jill told him. 'And my faith, of course. That's an enormous help.'

'Faith?' James stared blankly at her.

'I'm a lay preacher in our local group of churches. Didn't you know? I suppose you could say I have a strong if simple faith.'

'Even despite all that's happened?' he queried.

'All the more because of it,' Jill told him and because James looked even more baffled she found herself continuing, 'You see, I believe in a loving God who is in charge, even when it feels impossible. And I believe in a God who sees everything that's going on and cares about it and everybody involved, even when that seems most unlikely. And,' Jill took a deep breath and plunged on, 'I believe in a God who believes in justice, a God who won't let bad people get away with their wicked deeds, and who won't let innocent people suffer.'

James shook his head. 'You're lucky,' he muttered. He took her arm. 'Come on,' he said in his normal voice. 'Let me just grab my coat and we'll go and get some lunch.'

As they went downstairs, Jill commented, 'It's just as well you have that big sign pointing to the auction rooms, otherwise anyone could just come up here to the offices. We had a bit of a problem with that kind of thing at the school where I was head teacher. So many people nowadays just walk into a school – parents, suppliers, all kinds of reps... Well, what happened was that we had a bout of petty thefts – purses vanishing from handbags, that sort of thing. We had to put in a stricter system for letting people in to the admin part of the school and that soon put a stop to it.'

'That was bad luck,' James said. 'We've never had any problems like that. I suppose having to go upstairs would put off any impulse criminal.'

'Yes, I suppose so,' Jill agreed. It appeared that James did not know about the theft of Miss Schafer's handbag – or was he simply lying again?

It did not take long to sort out Jill's purchase, though she found herself having to explain about giving a different surname for her buyer's card when she came to pay with her credit card.

'I thought someone might recognise my surname as Hugo's so I felt a bit embarrassed. I wasn't planning on buying anything so I didn't think…'

At James's request a junior was sent hurriedly into the auction room to collect her purchase and bring it out to Jill. She was relieved to see that the lid was firmly on the box, which was clearly identified by its auction number. There was no need to explain to James what she had bought. She tucked the box safely into her handbag.

They went to a restaurant not far from the auction house.

'I used to bring Hugo here so I thought you'd like it,' James explained.

'That's kind of you,' Jill told him, adding 'I'm so glad you feel you can talk to me about him. So many people are embarrassed after a death. I suppose they're afraid I'll break down and cry all over them!'

'Well, I think by now I know you better than that,' James murmured with a smile and reached out to pat her hand.

Her skin crawled but Jill forced an answering smile on her face while she considered the pretty wife who had so innocently given her a lift into town, and the two daughters whose father apparently adored them. 'How can you?' she thought furiously. But she knew some silly men just needed to play away. She thought it was pathetic. In fact, looking at James, she decided he did look rather silly trying to smile seductively at her. It gave her extra boldness so she said, 'If you wouldn't mind talking about Hugo… It would be such a help…'

'Well, if you're sure…' James seemed a little put out. 'Let me get us something to drink, and then we'll need to order…'

The waiter appeared and James looked relieved to have to deal with drinks and food. But Jill was determined not to let him off the hook. When her drink arrived, she fixed him with her eyes and asked, 'So what was Hugo like to work with?'

James gulped down a sizeable portion of his wine. 'Well, obviously he was much more experienced than me…'

'I thought there was probably only around half a dozen years between you?' Jill probed.

'Yes, but I haven't been in this business very long.'

'You mean finance or the auction business?' Jill asked.

'The auction business.' James took another gulp of his wine. 'I only joined Aston Antiques about eighteen months ago.'

'Oh, I didn't know that. Where were you before?'

'I was Finance Director of a mobile phone company. Unfortunately it ran into difficulties – it's a very competitive market – and I was made redundant when it was taken over.'

'You must have been having kittens when you heard Russett & Thomson were taking over Aston Antiques, worrying that the same thing was going to happen,' Jill said, injecting warm sympathy into her voice.

'No, no,' James told her. 'You see, Hugo explained he was planning to retire next summer so not only was my job secure, but there was a promotion for me as Group Finance Director. It couldn't have been better. ...' He smiled easily and confidently, then a shadow seemed to pass across his face and he dragged his glass towards him and emptied it. Without asking Jill whether she would like a refill, he splashed more wine into his glass and downed it almost at once.

'So the take-over was a good thing for you,' Jill said brightly.

James seemed to jolt himself back to the present.

'The take-over? Oh, yes. You've seen our outfit. It works perfectly well, but it's small and doesn't offer much hope for the future. Whereas Russett & Thomson is a much bigger operation with an excellent reputation... Yes, the take-over was a good thing.' But his voice was flat and the meal proceeded with little further conversation and James drinking heavily.

'Lift to the station?' James asked perfunctorily as they left the restaurant.

Jill gave him a beady stare. 'I think we should both take taxis.'

He stared at her for a moment then started to laugh. 'You're probably right. I'm sorry. I don't know what came over me. Just a lot of pressure at the moment.'

'That's all right,' Jill told him. 'It gets to us all sometimes.'

'Too right. Now then,' he said, sounding a little more in control, 'do you need to get back immediately? Is there anything else you'd like to do while you're in Birmingham – a bit of shopping, maybe…?'

'Well, I did think I'd go to the hotel where Hugo used to stay when he came here.' Jill tried to harden her heart as she trotted out the lie. For a moment in the restaurant as she watched James slump into his dark mood, she had felt almost sorry for him. She continued with her carefully prepared story. 'The people who run it were such a lovely family and so good to him. I know he's supposed to have spent some of the times he said he was in Birmingham at that flat in Bath, with…. your secretary…'

James's eyes narrowed as he took this in. Watching his reaction, Jill decided to take the risk of pushing him further.

'I've got my diary here.' Jill patted her bag. 'I always wrote in the dates when Hugo said he'd be away. I just have this need to know how often he was lying to me. I'm sure they've got a register that would tell me. It may sound silly but it would really help me cope with all this if I knew it hadn't been very often. I would feel so much better…'

James's voice was rough as he cut across what she was saying. 'Wouldn't it be more fun to go shopping? Look, I don't have to get back to the office this afternoon. I'll come with you and show you the best places.'

'Shopping?' Jill echoed with surprise. 'I didn't think men liked shopping! No, no, I can't impose on you…'

'Well, how about an art gallery? I'm sure you'd enjoy that. Good idea to make the most of the opportunity while you're here. We've got some great galleries in Birmingham.' And moments later James was bundling Jill into a taxi and giving instructions for them to be taken to the Birmingham Museum and Art Gallery on Chamberlain Square.

Jill sat quietly beside him and then accompanied him without argument into the art gallery. As they walked round, James maintained a constant commentary on the Pre-Raphaelite paintings, bronze Buddhas and Egyptian mummies until Jill offered hesitantly that she was beginning to feel tired.

'Tea!' James exclaimed with enthusiasm. 'Just the thing! There's a rather splendid Edwardian tearoom here. We'll do that.' And he seized her arm again and began drawing her out of the gallery and through the Round Room to the busy tearoom. Bemused, Jill allowed herself to be guided to a table and settled into a chair. When the waitress arrived, James ordered tea and cakes for them both.

'You'll need a bit of sustenance before you get on the train,' he told her.

Jill checked her watch. 'Well, I do have time for tea,' she agreed 'but I feel guilty taking up so much of your time.'

'Not at all!' James insisted. 'It's a pleasure.'

Jill settled herself to sip tea and eat the sumptuous cakes with every appearance of enjoyment. Finally, she sat back and sighed.

'This was a good idea,' she told James. 'I love art galleries and we don't have many where I live, so this has been a treat. And a cream tea! I feel like a schoolgirl out for the day!'

James looked uncomfortable with her appreciation and simply shook his head.

'Look,' Jill continued. 'I don't want to be any more of a nuisance. I'll get a taxi straight back to the station. My train's due in half an hour. Then you can get back to the office. I reckon you could even pick up your car, you'll be ok to drive now. And nobody will have noticed you've been skiving off!'

'Well, if you're sure?'

'New Street Station isn't far from here, is it?' Jill asked.

'No, it's quite near but the one-way system makes it seem much further!'

'Then I'll be fine, and it would be a nuisance for you to have to come with me.' She rose and brushed the crumbs from her lap. 'But first I must find the ladies' room.'

As she rose from the table, she removed her make-up bag from her handbag, placed the handbag carefully on the table, and left her coat on the chair.

'I won't be a moment,' she said and hurried in the direction indicated by the sign on the far wall.

Once in the privacy of her cubicle in the ladies', Jill allowed herself to sag and relax. Something had certainly upset James at lunch. Was it talking about Hugo or the take-over? He had started knocking back the wine at that point. Then when she had mentioned the hotel and her diary, he had swept her up into this whirlwind of activity. Jill remembered Geoffrey's warning that she could be putting herself into danger. It was strange. She knew she was playing with fire, but she was feeling more alive than she had since Hugo died.

Coming out of the cubicle, she took time for a leisurely hand-wash and stood patiently to dry her hands under the air blower. Then she patted her hair and sternly told herself to calm down and look tired. The mirror above the basins showed someone far too cheerful and lively.

Leaving the ladies' room, she saw that James had picked up her coat and was waiting for her in the Round Room. Solicitously he helped her into it. She turned and managed to smile at him. Tall and elegant in his black winter coat over a smart grey suit, he could pass for the perfect escort.

'James, thank you for being so kind to me and giving me such a lovely day. It's made such a difference to me.'

'It's been a pleasure,' he told her but he seemed uneasy once again and in a hurry to go.

As they walked down the stairs to the exit, Jill stopped suddenly.

'My handbag! Drat, I must have left it in the ladies'. I do hope it's still there!' Without waiting for James's reaction, she turned and ran back upstairs to the ladies' room, where she waited for a few moments, gathering her thoughts. She had deliberately left her handbag on the table, having told James her diary with all the information about Hugo's business trips was inside, just to see what would happen. Too many items appeared to have gone missing without explanation – Hugo's desk diary, Penny's organiser, then Sylvia Schafer's handbag. So now Jill's handbag had gone missing too?

She hurried out again. 'It's not there! James, I did take it in with me, didn't I? Did I leave it at the table?'

James shook his head. 'I'm sorry, I can't remember.'

'Oh, what a nuisance!' Jill exclaimed as she hurried back to their table in the tearoom and made every sign of searching for the absent handbag.

A passing waitress stopped and enquired, 'Anything the matter?'

'My handbag,' Jill explained, in a fine show of distress. 'I can't find it!'

'If anyone picked it up, they'll have handed it in to Reception,' the waitress tried to reassure Jill. 'I'm sure you'll find it there.'

Jill grabbed James's arm. 'I don't know what I'll do if someone's stolen it. It was so silly just to leave it on the table.

I suppose I forgot I wasn't in Somerset where you can safely leave anything! Oh dear, and it's got my purse and my train ticket in it and…'

'I'm sure I can help you out on that,' James said, unmoving.

'Let's go to Reception and see if someone's handed it in,' Jill insisted and dragged him back to the Round Room and the Reception desk. There, Jill poured out her story.

'Yes, of course, madam,' the receptionist said. 'It was handed in just a few moments ago.' She reached under the desk and produced Jill's handbag.

Jill allowed herself to sag with relief.

'Oh, I am so glad! It's got my train ticket and everything…' She opened it hastily and probed around, bringing out her wallet and checking inside. 'Yes, it's all here!' She turned to James with a beaming smile. 'All's well that ends well!' she told him. 'Thank you so much,' she told the receptionist. 'I'm so grateful! I'd really have been in a mess without it!'

James seemed rather tight-lipped as they left so Jill chattered happily about the art they had seen as they hurried out to the pavement outside. There, James hastily flagged down a couple of taxis.

'I hope we haven't made you late for your train,' he told her.

'I'll be fine!' she reassured him. 'A run along the platform will be good exercise after those cream cakes!'

He waved her off without any further conversation and, Jill noted, this time no affectionate farewell kiss. She was glad when the taxi moved away, leaving her alone, and she leaned back in her seat with a sigh of relief.

'New Street Station, love?' the taxi driver checked.

'That's right,' Jill said as she opened her handbag. She grinned with sudden delight as she saw that her diary was missing – just as well she'd copied those dates on to her computer – but the smile faded as she noticed the lid of the cufflinks box had been knocked off. She pulled the box out and tipped the cufflinks out into her hand. They were all there.

But James would have seen them and realised she had been lying about buying jewellery for herself. Worse, if it had been James who had put the cufflinks into the sale, he would know that they were Hugo's. And he would know that she knew too.

CHAPTER 23

Jill had arranged to meet Ed George at the coffee bar in the station complex. As she got nearer, she realised she did not know what he looked like and hesitated on the threshold, looking around her. She was relieved when a large rumpled man rose from a table and brandished a copy of that day's *Informer*. When she smiled with relief, he waved her over.

'Jill?'

She hurried towards him and he pulled out a chair for her.

'Hi, I'm Ed. It's good to meet you,' he said. And after they had dealt with the introductory formalities, he enquired, 'Coffee? Tea?'

'I think I've had enough tea to sink a battleship!' Jill told him. 'I've had a busy day – much busier than I planned.' And she proceeded to tell him how she had tracked down the unfamiliar address on the bank statement, and discovered not only that it was James's but that he had a charming wife and two teenage daughters who thought the world of him.

'Then I had a wild idea,' she confessed.

'How wild?' Ed asked disapprovingly.

'Very,' Jill admitted, though her eyes danced with mischief. 'I took a taxi to Aston Antiques and went to an auction there. I thought I'd be safe because it's Wednesday so James would be at the Ilminster office…'

'But?'

'Yes, there is a "but",' Jill agreed and told him how she had discovered two pairs of Hugo's cufflinks in the sale and had bid for them, having to attract the auctioneer's attention – and, via the cctv, James's.

'So he wasn't in Ilminster,' Ed said flatly.

'No. And what's worse, when he spotted me on the cctv, he came to check that it was me and then, after a lightning tour of the building, whisked me off for lunch. That's when it got really interesting.' She related how James had reacted to her plan to visit Aston Towers and check on Hugo's visits there.

'And he nicked my diary when I was in the ladies' loo!' she said cheerfully.

'But that's evidence!' Ed protested.

'I've copied everything on to my computer so I haven't lost any data. The thing that does worry me is that I think he saw the cufflinks. When I got them, they were in a box with a tightly fitting lid – but when I checked my handbag, the lid had come off. I'd told James I'd bought some jewellery. Now he'll know I've got the cufflinks. If he put them in the sale…'

'Somebody did,' Ed said. 'That's for sure. I'm afraid you may have blown your cover, buying the cufflinks…'

'I couldn't leave them for someone else!' Jill protested.

'I can see that, but the thing is you lied to James, and probably pretty convincingly!'

Jill grinned at that, but Ed's next words chilled her.

'He won't think you are such an innocent any more. He may even feel threatened. I think you need to be careful.'

'Yes, I suppose so,' Jill agreed thoughtfully. 'I do think he's panicking, otherwise he wouldn't do anything as obvious as steal the diary. Especially when we know Hugo's desk diary was "lost" and then Penny's organiser was stolen.'

'True.'

'Anyway, enough about my exploits. How did you get on with Miss Schafer?'

'Well, she's not *Miss* Schafer for a start. It's Mrs. There's a husband tucked away somewhere. She's an interesting lady, that,' Ed said thoughtfully. 'She's a bit-part actress. Schafer isn't her real name. I couldn't get out of her what it was but it'll be easy enough to find out. She temps between acting jobs and that's how she came to be at Aston Antiques just as the take-over was in progress.'

'Interesting,' Jill said and repeated what James had said, the evening after their dinner at Little Barwick, about the woman on the Answermachine being 'heavily into the theatre'. 'So at least he was telling the truth about that.' She hesitated then plunged on. 'Did you find out anything about... her relationship with Hugo?'

'Well, she does claim to have had a fling with your husband. Said he'd asked her to fix up the flat for them to use and so on.'

'I don't believe any of that any more,' Jill told him firmly. 'Nothing I've found out so far backs it up in any way. It looks like a set-up to me. And don't you think it's odd that the bank statements on that account were sent to James's address?'

'Yes, that is odd. Though I suppose theoretically your husband could have asked James to cover for him so you wouldn't know?'

'I don't think they were on those sorts of terms,' Jill replied thoughtfully. 'James seemed to have seen Hugo as rather senior to him. In fact he got a bit moody, hitting the bottle rather, when we talked about it.'

'Now that is something Mrs Schafer mentioned,' Ed put in. 'She said James seemed to be losing his grip. She reckons that basically he's out of his depth at work now that he has to cope without your husband. Seems he's new to the auction business.'

Jill was able to back that up. 'Yes, James told me that himself.'

'Well,' Ed continued, 'Mrs Schafer also said that James is drinking heavily. In fact, she said it was becoming a bit of a problem at work. She told me she was looking very seriously for another job. Reckoned her current situation wasn't a good place to be. She seemed to be rather worried about it all. In fact, I'd say she's pretty anxious, even a bit scared of him.'

'Of James?' Jill queried that. 'His wife says he's really an old softie…'

'Well, you know what they say – an angel at home, a devil at work.'

'That can be true, I suppose,' Jill considered. There had been moments with James when she had felt a sudden stab of fear. She remembered particularly the evening when she had listened to the Answermachine message and James had shouted at her in fury. 'I did wonder whether there was something going on between Sylvia Schafer and James Wheatley?'

'I wouldn't think so. There's no love lost there at all. In fact she made it very plain that she has no time for him. She talked about some auditions she has coming up. I reckon she wants to get away as soon as possible. Don't think she'll hang around for long.'

'Well, James seemed to be in an equal hurry to get away from me this afternoon – once I'd got my handbag back!'

'If he did take your diary, and saw the cufflinks, he'll have a lot to be worried about. He must know now that you're on to him,' Ed pointed out.

'True. Oh, well,' Jill said, adding 'Poor James.'

'Poor James?' Ed echoed. 'This is the man who may be at the bottom of this farrago of lies about your husband. Or worse.'

'Worse?'

'Surely you realise that if there was no affair and no sordid little love nest, then what reason would your husband have for committing suicide? If it was suicide.'

Jill shivered. 'What are you saying?'

'I'm not saying anything. But I think you should be careful, just in case…'

In the sudden silence between them, the tannoy announcement for Jill's train was very loud.

'Come on,' Ed said. 'Let's get you on that train and safely home.'

He accompanied her to the locker where she retrieved her overnight bag and walked silently with her along the busy approach to the platform where her train was due to arrive.

As they stood at the edge of the platform, Ed turned to her and put a hand on her arm.

'You will keep in touch, won't you?' he asked. 'If anything happens to worry you, or if James turns up, all you have to do…'

His words were drowned out by the roar of the high-speed train arriving in the station. With his hand on her arm, he felt Jill sway forwards suddenly and as he grabbed at her coat to pull her back to safety, he caught a glimpse of a black-sleeved arm. Then it was gone in the crush.

Jill sagged against him.

'Someone pushed me,' she croaked in shock. 'I felt a hand on my back…'

There came the sudden blue-white explosion of a flashbulb and with that Jill fainted at Ed's feet.

The crowd parted as he called to them to give her air. Instantly, she came to and was staring at him in puzzlement.

'What happened?' she demanded. 'I didn't faint, did I? How revoltingly girly!'

Ed began to laugh. He gathered her into his arms and held her close for a warm comforting moment, his laughter rumbling through his chest, and Jill joined in weakly.

'Come on,' he said. 'I'll come with you as far as Bath. At least I'll be sure you've got that far safely. I can change there on to the London train. We can talk on the way.'

In a swift move, he grabbed her overnight bag and helped her onto the train, finding them seats in an empty foursome round a table.

'I think you could probably do with a drink,' he suggested.

'Too right!' she agreed, letting herself fall back into the seat and closing her eyes.

'I'll be back in one second,' he told her and hurried to the buffet carriage, calling after him, 'Now don't go anywhere!'

Jill chuckled softly. She was in no state to go anywhere and they both knew it. She let her breathing slow, counting the breaths till her heart rate was back to normal and ticking along steadily. She took a deep breath and opened her eyes.

Ed was standing there with a couple of plastic tumblers and two miniatures of spirits in his hand.

'You look a bit better,' he said and sat down, carefully setting his purchases on the table between them. 'Whisky?' he enquired.

'Wonderful. Never drink the stuff but I reckon I deserve to start now!'

'Take it easy then. It's fierce.'

Taking him at his word, she carefully took a sip of the golden liquid, feeling the sharpness of the fumes hitting her nostrils. And at once she was coughing as the fire caught the back of her throat.

'Easy!' Ed said.

Jill laughed and took another sip, letting the heat slink down her throat and into her stomach where it glowed like an internal hot water bottle.

She smiled. 'Better. That was a good idea.'

'Now,' Ed began. 'What exactly happened back there?'

'I told you. Just as the train was coming in, I felt a hand on my back. Whoever it was gave me an almighty shove. I lost my balance…' She looked at Ed, the fear back in her eyes. 'If you hadn't been there – if you hadn't grabbed me – I'd have fallen under that train!' She shuddered and closed her eyes.

Ed reached over and nudged the tumbler in her hand. 'Have another sip of that Scotch. You need it.'

Jill obeyed and let the liquid fire drive away the chill that had invaded her bones as she thought of what might have happened.

'So, are we agreed it wasn't an accident?' Ed asked abruptly. 'Not simply someone in the crush just catching you off balance?'

Jill shook her head vehemently. 'Definitely not. It was deliberate. There was that hand on my back, then when the train got near, a shove…'

'Right. So we need to assume that someone wants you out of the way.'

Jill looked up from the plastic tumbler of whisky, her eyes wide but her face set and calm. 'Yes. It certainly looks like that,' she agreed.

'Which means you're getting a bit close to the truth…'

'About why Hugo died…'

'Or was killed.'

Jill sipped the last of the whisky, taking her time, thinking. 'You said earlier maybe it wasn't suicide?'

Ed nodded.

'I couldn't understand it, myself,' Jill told him quietly. 'Hugo was no coward. He'd face up to anybody or anything!'

'And?'

'And now I know he had nothing to do with that sordid flat in Bath. Every time he was meant to be away from home, he was staying at the Aston Towers Hotel. I've got proof of that. I never did believe that he would have an affair with that woman. I think it was all made up.'

'And if it was all made up?'

'That probably includes the embezzlement, too,' Jill said. 'I'll never believe Hugo did anything like that. It just wasn't in his nature. And anyway, he didn't need to embezzle to get the money for the flat. He could have covered it on his credit card and I'd never have known. So that must be part of it too.' She shook her head. 'No. I think it was all made up.'

'But by whom? And why?'

'I don't know for sure yet,' Jill confessed 'but it looks like James is definitely in there somewhere. He was really rattled today.'

'And his secretary says he's losing his grip, drinking heavily…'

'Could it have been James who pushed me?' Jill asked slowly.

'All I saw was an arm in a heavy black coat,' Ed said.

Jill thought back to when she had last seen James. He had been wearing a coat, a heavy black winter coat. She remembered him putting it on the back of one of the chairs in the art gallery tearoom. He had been wearing it as he stood waiting for her to come out of the ladies'.

Her face told the truth.

'James?' Ed asked.

Jill nodded.

'He was wearing a heavy black coat today.'

CHAPTER 24

✣

Jill yawned.

'Darling, you must go to bed. You've had a horrid day,' her mother scolded her affectionately.

Jill nodded wearily. It had been a thoroughly exhausting day and she was still struggling to make sense of it all. As she climbed the stairs to the guestroom in her mother's house, she reflected on how kind Ed had been. It had been his idea that she stay over at her mother's in Bath where she had left her car rather than go home to her own house in Somerton.

'You'll be safer there,' he had told her bluntly. 'I assume that James doesn't know where your mother lives?'

'No,' she had assured him. 'I think I've only said she lives in Bath. And of course Mum has a different surname to mine, so she wouldn't be easy to track down.'

Ed had nodded, apparently satisfied with her answer, but then had insisted on finding a taxi and accompanying her to the door. He had waited till she was safely indoors before the taxi drove him away.

'Who was that?' her mother enquired. 'He looked nice…'

And when Jill had told her everything, she had murmured approvingly, 'Good man. I'm glad there's someone to look out for you.'

'There's God looking after me,' Jill reminded her wearily.

'Yes, dear, of course,' her mother replied sharply, 'but it's nice to have a real live human male on the ground when you need him – and it seems to me that at this moment in time, you need a good strong male to look after you. I just wish he could stop you placing yourself in danger!'

'Oh, Mum!' Jill protested, 'I'm not an infant, or some silly bimbo!'

'No, dear, I know that, but I've said what I said and I mean it.'

It was at that point that Jill gave in to the exhaustion that was beginning to overwhelm her and yawned.

Tucked up cosily in bed, she was asleep the minute her head hit the pillow.

Thursday dawned crisp and bright so Jill decided a brisk walk would do her good. Bundled up in warm clothes, she headed into Bath after breakfast, striding out and enjoying the gentle warmth of the winter sun on her skin and its enhancing glow on the buildings around her.

She decided to buy a newspaper and read it in leisurely fashion while she had a cappuccino but when she browsed through the papers in the nearest newsagent's she found herself face to face with a photograph of herself on the front page of a tabloid paper. The headline screamed: DISTRAUGHT WIDOW'S SUICIDE ATTEMPT.

Trembling with anger, she bought the paper and hurried back to her mother's house where she could read the offending article in privacy. Her mother found her in the kitchen, her knuckles white as she gripped a coffee mug fiercely.

'I thought I heard you come back,' she began, then seeing Jill's rigid features, asked, 'What's wrong?'

Jill flapped the offending newspaper at her.

'Look at this! It's dreadful. But what can I do?'

Jill's mother took the paper from her and read the article. In blaring detail, it told how Jill's suicide attempt, by trying to throw herself under the Birmingham high-speed train to Bath, had been unsuccessful. It went on to give full details of Hugo's suicide, embezzlement from the firm, affair with Sylvia Schafer and so on, and concluded that it was quite common for those left behind by a suicide – the spouse or partner – to also commit suicide within eighteen months of the first death.

Jill's mother threw it on to the kitchen table and sat down beside Jill, taking one hand in hers.

'You wouldn't think of doing anything like that, would you, darling?' she asked with quiet concern.

'No, Mum, I wouldn't,' Jill told her. 'Anyway, I'm not your average suicide survivor. I'm not traumatised by grief. I'm *angry*! Maybe the grief will hit me later – but not now. Not yet. I've got things to do first. I'm sure now that there's something fishy going on. I didn't try some stupid suicide attempt. Someone pushed me, I told you. And Ed caught me and pulled me back. He knows I didn't try to jump! This is another set-up – like the rubbish in Ed's paper about Hugo and the sleazy love nest!'

Jill's mother picked up the paper again and looked at the photograph.

'You're not looking your best there,' she commented.

Jill stared at her for a moment, then the incongruity of her mother's statement hit them both and they began to laugh. Relieved that Jill was again her normal self, her mother rose and refilled their coffee mugs.

'I remember the flash bulb,' Jill said thoughtfully. 'Then I fainted. Just for a moment. That must be how they got the picture.'

'*They?*'

'Whoever is responsible for all of this. I don't want to say yet – I'm not completely sure – but I know I'm getting close…'

'Darling, please be careful. Whoever it is sounds extremely dangerous. If they've made one attempt…'

'Yes, I know. But I've got to be sure before I can go to the police.'

'But how seriously are the police going to take your ideas after this?' Her mother indicated the paper and its mocking headline – a sentiment that was echoed by Ed when Jill rang him a little later.

'Yeah, I reckon that's probably the point. It's all about discrediting you as a witness. The police will think you've just got a little unhinged with grief,' he told her.

Jill snorted.

'I know, I know,' Ed soothed. 'Anyone less unhinged is hard to imagine… But look at it from their point of view: hysterical irrational relatives with conspiracy theories are pretty common and a real nuisance.'

'Well, thank you!' Jill said, then ever practical, asked, 'Look, I know they've chosen your fiercest rival to put this garbage in, but is there any way we can find out who sent in the stuff this time?'

'It may be my paper's fiercest rival,' Ed said, 'but journalists are pack animals and they all hang out at the same watering holes. The byline is my old mate Gary's. I'll check it out with him when I see him in the pub at lunchtime. Let me find out what he can tell me and I'll get back to you as soon as I can. By the way, where are you going to be? I think it would be much safer if you could stay at your mother's for a while…'

'I know. I probably will stay,' Jill agreed. 'She's quite happy to have me and my neighbour is feeding my cat. But I hate the feeling of being driven out of my own home.'

'The alternative is worse. Back in your own place, you could be in serious danger.'

'I know. All right. I'll stay put for a while.'

'You don't mind, Mum, do you?' she checked with her mother after she had put the phone down.

'Not at all. I agree with that man. You're much safer here.'

But Jill was restless. In her own home, there was always plenty to do, in the house or in the garden, and while Barney would be perfectly well looked after by the neighbour, he would be vociferous in his disapproval when she finally returned home. Meanwhile she felt purposeless, and her mind started going over what she had found out and trying to make sense of it.

She was convinced now that the story about Hugo having an affair with Sylvia Schafer was completely untrue. She could prove that he had not spent any nights at the Bath flat, and it was not his signature on either the lease document or the cheque which had covered the deposit and the first month's rent. It was the same forged signature on the new driving licence that had been provided as proof of his identity. The only person the agent had dealt with in fixing the let had been

Sylvia Schafer, James's secretary – the secretary who was now frightened and desperate to get away.

The person who had forged Hugo's signature on the lease and the deposit cheque had to be the same person who had forged Hugo's signature when opening the bank account in Birmingham. So at the heart of it was someone who had set it all up in Hugo's name as part of a carefully organised plan to discredit him.

She could not believe that Hugo would have stolen money from his own firm. In any case, the amount involved was ridiculously small, just enough to cover the deposit on the Bath flat and one month's rent. As she had told Ed, Hugo could have covered that easily on one of his credit cards. She added into the equation that the statements on the bank account into which Hugo had supposedly put the money he had embezzled had gone to James's home address in Birmingham. As Ed had suggested, a sympathetic friend who was helping him cover up an affair might assist in this way – but Jill was sure that Hugo and James had not been on such close terms.

She had thought it very kind of James to persuade the firm to let him investigate the embezzlement and draw a line under it all. To have brought in the police would have meant freezing both Hugo's and Jill's bank accounts and would have created enormous problems for her. How kind, she had thought at the time. But now she wondered. If James had known the whole story was false, he would not have been willing to risk letting the police get involved in any investigation.

There were two big questions, though, that Jill could not answer. Why would anyone want to set up Hugo like that and discredit him? And why would he have committed suicide if it was all a pack of lies?

And that was when the third question that had been lurking at the back of her mind came into sharp focus. Ed had suggested it, even Geoffrey had mentioned it as a logical possibility, but she had been shoving it away into the back of her mind every time it surfaced. It was too big a leap to consider seriously. But now that an attempt had been made on her own life, just as she was beginning to get at the facts, she had to face it. If Hugo had had no real reason to commit suicide, then had he been murdered?

CHAPTER 25

❈

'I'M GOING TO go home,' Jill announced. 'Yes, I know – you and Ed have both kindly pointed out that I may be putting myself in serious danger but I can't let myself be imprisoned... Oh, Mum, I don't mean that the way it sounded!' Jill rushed to apologise as she heard herself express in such uncomplimentary terms how she was feeling. '*You're* not imprisoning me. It's being forced out of my own home and into hiding that I hate.'

'It's all right, darling, I know what you mean,' her mother reassured her. 'But isn't there anyone you could have to stay? Someone who could watch out for you, just in case? I know I'd be much easier in my mind...'

'I don't want anyone to stay,' Jill said firmly. 'I'd much prefer to be on my own. I need space to think this thing through to its logical conclusion. But I'll tell Geoffrey and Monica that I'm home, and Jenneva Rawlings. They'll keep an eye out for me, I'm sure, and check regularly that I'm all right.'

'If you're sure, darling.' Her mother was unconvinced. 'You know I'll worry.'

'I am sure. All I need is just a little more evidence then – tabloid or no tabloid trying to discredit me – I'll go to the police and hand it all over to them.'

By the time she had thrown her overnight bag into her car, her mother's repetition of 'Do be careful!' and 'Are you sure?' was wearing thin. Jill forced a smile and hugged her.

'Try not to worry. I'll be fine, honest! I've got good friends and I'm pretty sensible,' she assured her mother, feeling guilty that she was so glad to be waving goodbye and setting off back to Somerset and her own peaceful home.

As she drove, she considered her mother's obvious concerns. If she asked, Jenneva might come to stay but what could Jenneva do? Feisty she might be but she would be no match for a determined killer. And Geoffrey and Monica, they had their own lives to lead and could not mount a vigilante squad to protect her, even if they believed her!

No, she had to do this on her own. After all, what did she have to lose? Hugo was dead. She had been gently eased into early retirement from work. Although she loved her mother and sister, they could manage perfectly well without her. There was Barney the cat. He would miss her but someone would take him in. After all, he was well-used to being fed by her neighbour when Jill stayed at her mother's.

Truthfully there really was not very much that she herself would miss greatly, now that Hugo was dead. Any kind of meaningful life without him seemed unbearably impossible. It was remarkable how she had not noticed how their lives had become interwoven into one strand while he was alive. Now, she felt only half-alive – or less – without him. The future no longer existed as a friendly place just up in front with things to look forward to. Instead it was a great big blank brick wall with nothing on the other side except long plodding years of emptiness leading to her own inevitable death – and, hopefully, reunion with Hugo.

She shook herself. She was becoming self-pitying and maudlin! This would not do. Sternly, she forced herself to concentrate on her driving and turned on the radio to try and distract herself, even making herself sing along when something she knew was played.

The phone was ringing when she got in. She was not surprised to find the caller was Ed. An irate Ed.

'You are out of your mind!' he told her forcefully. 'Wasn't one attempt on your life enough?'

'I know,' she said, with a sigh. 'But I felt penned in at my mother's. There are things I need to find out, things I need to do here… Anyway, what did you manage to find out from your friend?'

'It was done exactly the same as last time,' Ed told her. 'Gary got an envelope with the photograph in it and typed back-up information.'

'Nothing to say who it was from?'

'Nothing,' Ed growled. 'These people know what they're doing. I don't like it. You're setting yourself up like a target…'

'Well, I'm not too keen on that either but I think I have to be here,' Jill told him. 'I promise I'll be very careful and I'll make sure my friends know where I am and what I'm doing.'

'I still don't like it,' Ed said. 'This whole thing has moved up a gear. Whoever you're dealing with is panicking, taking risks. That makes it even less safe for you to be stirring things up.'

'Look, Ed!' Jill told him firmly, 'I can't just give up now, as if I'd been scared into silence. Not when I feel I'm so close to the answer.'

'Maybe that's what your husband decided,' Ed said grimly. 'And look what happened to him.'

She thought about that carefully as she unpacked her overnight bag.

'Was that how it was?' she asked Hugo, directing her question in the general direction of the urn on the bedroom mantelpiece. 'Did you find out something and someone – was it James? – decided you had to be silenced?'

It made sense. As Group Finance Director, Hugo would have examined very carefully the books of the company they were taking over. He would have been sure to spot if anything were amiss.

But surely he would have mentioned it to her? He shared his life with her, told her what was going on in his committees, at work, everywhere. They were married, after all!

Maybe he had not been sure. Or maybe it was something he had discovered only in the last month or so of his life, when everything had got a bit hectic – both with the take-over and, she had to admit, in her own life at school. Maybe she had been too busy… She remembered the Parents Evening just days before Hugo's death. She had not been able to sit down and listen to him at any time during that week.

A pang of guilt shot through her like a knife. Guilt! That was all she needed. Trying to focus on the facts, Jill went downstairs and checked her notes. The lease of the Bath flat had only started two weeks before Hugo's death. Whatever Hugo had found out, it had triggered this farrago of smear and deception only two or three weeks before his death.

She turned it over in her mind. She could not imagine what might have happened to alert Hugo to something wrong at Aston Antique Sales. Might he have mentioned something to anyone else? She rang Geoffrey.

'Jill! How are you? Are you in hospital?'

It took Jill a moment to work out what he was talking about.

'You should read more upmarket papers,' she told him. 'The tabloids are full of rubbish!'

'What do you mean?'

'I did not attempt suicide. I was pushed. And before you say I'm imagining it, I can assure you there was someone with me who can vouch for me!'

'Good gracious, Jill! I told you not to meddle…'

'Well, I'm meddling and it's bringing the nasties out of the woodwork.'

'I don't like this.'

'That's the third time today someone's said that to me!'

'Have you actually found out more?'

'Yes, I have' and Jill told him about the Patel family's evidence that Hugo had always stayed at the Aston Towers Hotel when he was away from home, so there was no time available for him to use the Bath flat. She added the details from the bank manager about the bank account with James's address for receipt of statements.

'It looks like this man, James Wheatley, is at the back of all this,' Geoffrey said slowly. 'If you'll promise me that you won't do any more meddling, I'll have a word with someone I know in the police, see if they'll look at what you've discovered. I'm not promising anything…'

'Neither am I,' Jill told him. 'First, there are a couple of things I need to know and I think you may be able to help.'

'Oh, Jill!' Geoffrey groaned. 'I really wish you wouldn't!'

'I know – and I wish I didn't have to, but I do. In any case, can't you just start the ball rolling with your police friend?'

'I suppose I could. He won't be happy to have you digging things up though. The police don't like amateurs getting in the way.'

'I suppose not, but I won't rest till I understand what happened,' Jill told him 'and I'm the person best placed to do the finding out. So: can you remember anything different about Hugo in the weeks before his death, anything up to say four weeks before? Did he mention anything unusual that had happened at work?'

'Well, we had that tremendous bust-up, but we made it up as usual. Hugo seemed his old self.' Geoffrey paused.

Jill thought with a grin that she could almost hear the cogs connecting and start to turn, slowly.

'Except,' Geoffrey continued thoughtfully 'for the night he came to the office. I told you about that. He was very jumpy, looking over his shoulder all the time as though he was worried he might be seen talking to me. That was very odd. Not like him at all. And there was that car circling the Market Place.'

'Ah yes, the black Range Rover…'

'I thought nothing of it. It's a very common make around here. Living on the Levels, people need four-wheel drive for when it floods. Anyway, Hugo rushed off at high speed. I thought that was because he was going to be late for meeting you after your Parents Evening do.'

'Yes, I remember,' Jill said. 'But he wasn't late. He was sitting in my office waiting for me, reading a book, when I got there. It was me who was late. I'd overrun as usual!'

There was silence, then, 'Jill, I am sorry about all this and I'll have a word with my friend. Maybe they'll be willing to pick it up and save you putting yourself on the line. All this ferreting out of the details of Hugo's last days can't be helping you. You've got to deal with your grief and then…'

'Move on?' Jill supplied the words for him with a wry smile. 'Yes, but not till I've got to the bottom of this. I want to clear Hugo's name. Then I'll have a whopping great memorial service for him and a party, and then I'll move on, I promise!'

CHAPTER 26

✥

'You're crazy,' Jenneva Rawlings told her. She leaned across the table and helped herself to a chocolate chip cookie, holding it up to admire it before biting into it. 'But I'm not surprised. I can perfectly understand. I'd probably do the same if it were me. So, what can I do to help?'

'Bless you, Jenn,' Jill said warmly. 'What I need is to find out what it was that triggered all this and I reckon it happened a little while before that flat in Bath was rented. That was the beginning of the blackening of Hugo's name.' She had told Jenneva about the forged signatures on the copy documents now securely locked away in Geoffrey's office safe.

'So maybe Hugo had found out something and let – James? – know he knew?'

'That's what I think, and it's got to be something on the Finance side. That's the area he would be paying attention to.'

'But his secretary's been "let go" and James is running that side now, right?'

'Right.'

'So you won't get anywhere asking any questions there?' Jenn asked, sipping her coffee thoughtfully.

'Correct and convenient.' Jill paused and added, 'Well, I have been in touch with Penny. She was Hugo's secretary. I'm sure the theft of her electronic organiser was no accident. We'd just been checking the dates when Hugo was supposed to be away from home. I'd got my diary out and it must have been pretty obvious what we were doing. I'm sure someone – James, I suppose – saw us. We were at Monty's in Taunton for lunch and it was very busy.'

'Yes, I can see it could have been deliberate,' Jenneva agreed. 'It's a bit conspiracy theory, though, don't you think?'

'The whole thing is!' Jill protested. 'But I'm beginning to find out who is at the bottom of it. I rang Penny to see if she could remember anything unusual that happened in the last few weeks before Hugo's death but she's on holiday. Gone off to the sunshine and I don't blame her.'

'Is there nobody else in the firm you could talk to?'

'It's more like who else in the firm would be prepared to talk to me!' Jill said. 'You'd think it was me who had done something scandalous the way I've been dropped. No more dinner party invites for me from the great and the good…'

'Like who?'

'Whom,' Jill corrected absently.

'Schoolmarm!' Jenn retaliated cheerfully. 'Go on then, whom?'

'Well, I always thought Hugo and Jim Russett were good friends…'

'He's the Managing Director, right?'

'That's right. They built up the business together, virtually from scratch. They always said they made a good team. Hugo was the financial wizard who got the money to start the business up and then made sure it all ran like clockwork.'

Jenneva's ironically raised eyebrow provoked Jill to defend Hugo. 'Running an auction house is complicated from the finance side. It's not just the hammer price on each item – sometimes five figures or more – that you have to keep track of. There's also the buyer's premium, then commission and any expenses like insurance that need to be deducted before the vendor gets paid, and there's always VAT of course! It's fiddly and you need to have it well organised to work smoothly.'

'OK, more complicated that I thought,' Jenn acknowledged.

Jill continued, 'It was Jim who had the eye for fine art and antiques. And he had the manner that encouraged people to place really good quality items with him for auction. He's also a brilliant auctioneer. The way he can coax bids is amazing! I used to love going to the special sales days and watching.'

'Then that's what you've got to do,' Jenn announced.

'What? Go to an auction? Look what happened the last time I went to an auction. And anyway, I'm not sure I could bear it, being there again, And everyone would stare…'

'Listen, sweetie,' Jenn told her firmly. 'I know all about being shunned for having a scandalous… past … and present!' She laughed. 'The only way to survive is to brazen it out. If people don't like it, that's their problem!'

'I'd be surprised if they'd even let me in!'

'First of all, they can't stop you. It's a public sale, right?'

'Right.' But Jill did not sound convinced.

'And second, I'll come with you.'

Jill hesitated. Having Jenn with her would bolster her courage.

'But what for?' she asked in a small voice. 'What reason could I have for being there?'

'Well, we're not going to buy anything, if that's what you thought! You're going to brazen it out and confront old Jim Russett. In a public place like that, he can't get away and he can't ignore you. The pair of us can corner him and then you can tell him what you've found out so far. Once he realises there's something really odd about it all, surely he'll want to get it cleared up? You can ask if he remembers anything that might help.'

Jill thought about it. Fine art and antiques sales were usually held on Thursdays. Since James only visited the Ilminster office on Wednesdays she was unlikely to bump into him, although his presence in the Birmingham office on the Wednesday she had been there had been an unexpected change of routine and an unpleasant surprise. As she considered the situation, it was clear that Jim Russett was the only person she could talk to who might have some idea of whatever had happened to trigger this whole nightmare.

Hugo and Jim had been friends, she was sure of that. Genuine friends, not just work colleagues who were able to rub along for the sake of the business. She had been hurt by the curt little note on the condolence card but perhaps Jim had been as shocked by Hugo's death and apparent betrayal as she had.

Jenn was right. It was time to come out of hiding and face up to all these people she used to know. One of them held the key to what had happened and she was determined to find out what it was.

'OK,' she told Jenneva. 'Let's do it. Tomorrow morning at ten o'clock and leave your chequebook and credit cards behind. You'll be tempted, I'm sure of it, and I don't want to be held responsible!'

CHAPTER 27

IT WAS SURPRISING how much comfort there was in being somewhere so familiar. Jill gazed affectionately at the long row of smartly painted buildings with the big glossy sign 'Russett & Thomson, Fine Art & Antiques Auctioneers', as Jenneva swung her Range Rover into the car park and flirted with the attendant before handing over the £1 fee.

'You're incorrigible! That poor man!' Jill teased her.

'Poor man?' Jenn echoed. 'No man needs your sympathy. They're all bastards and fair game.'

Not Jill's point of view, she had to admit. In fact, having met James's wife, she even felt a little sorry for him. Something terrible must have gone wrong in his life if he was willing to endanger what looked like a loving family. He was certainly panicking now. She grabbed her handbag and caught her breath and her courage as she followed Jenn into the reception area.

'Hi!' Jenn said breezily. 'Can I have a catalogue and how do I get a bid card?'

The smilingly efficient woman behind the counter handed over a catalogue and rapidly produced forms for Jenn to sign and a large, clearly numbered bid card. Jill felt uncomfortable. She was sure the woman recognised her. She thought she saw her eyes flicker over her and back a couple of times. As they turned to leave, the woman said hesitantly, 'It's good to see you again, Mrs Leiston. We were all terribly sorry…'

'Thank you,' Jill said, touched by the woman's kindness. Jenn tugged her arm. 'Come on!' So she smiled and allowed herself to be dragged away.

The main auction room was as sumptuous as she remembered, with its deep wine-coloured walls showing off the furniture and paintings to perfection. High lighting and tracked spotlights picked out the fine porcelain and sculptures. Glass cases held sparkling crystal and gleaming silver.

'Ooh, lovely!' Jenn breathed. 'Let's just have a little lustful browse!'

'You're impossible.' Jill had to laugh.

'True! Thank you!' and Jenn pulled her towards a display of Clarice Cliff.

'Now, I can't stand the stuff myself – a bit crude and vulgar for my taste, but it's fetching a fortune these days. Moorcroft's more my line or good studio pottery – Bernard Leach, for example.'

Jenn led Jill round the displays, pointing to this, denigrating that, and maintaining such a flow of delightful and quite knowledgeable chatter that Jill began to relax and enjoy herself.

'You know, we ought to have done this ages ago. You make a wonderful guide!'

'I've always been interested in this stuff,' Jenn said. 'In fact, I went to Art School way back when and I've started painting again. So much more interesting than boring old farming.' She gave a dismissive flap of her hand. 'Let's grab a coffee and come back and get the best seats before the hordes arrive.'

The café-bistro was situated behind the auction room, on two floors with a viewing gallery. Everything was spotless and good quality and Jill could not help comparing her surroundings with the shabby down-at-heel appearance of the Birmingham auction rooms.

They carried their mugs of coffee back to the main auction room and seated themselves on a comfortable sofa a decorous couple of rows back from the auctioneer's rostrum. A group of staff was busily correcting details on duplicated sheets, checking things on a computer, and organising places by the phones.

'This looks like fun. Oh, I fancy that young man over there. He looks just my type.' Jenn gestured towards a young man smartly dressed in a dark suit, typing something into the computer on the desk below the rostrum.

'Naughty!' Jill protested. 'He's young enough to be your son.'

'Sons we don't talk about,' Jenn warned her darkly.

Remembering the acrimonious split between Jenn and her only son, Jill hastened to apologise.

'Don't worry. Water under the bridge,' Jenn told her airily but Jill felt sure she was pretending.

Soon, the auctioneer climbed up into the rostrum, accompanied by a woman who sat down next to him with a copy of the sale details. A bang on the gavel, 'Ladies and Gentlemen!' and the sale had begun. A pretty young girl in a neat black skirt, white blouse and bright pink jacket moved around the room and held up items for sale or indicated which was currently on offer.

In the familiar atmosphere, Jill relaxed and watched the proceedings. The auctioneer was indeed Jim Russett but he looked quite a lot older, as though the preceding months had taken their toll. Still, he worked his way through the 400 items at considerable speed, teasing bids out of seemingly unwilling buyers and producing some excellent prices.

Jenn, marking prices down alongside estimates in the catalogue, murmured, 'He *is* good, isn't he? And they know their stuff.'

For a moment Jill basked in the praise, then a sudden emptiness descended as she remembered she was no longer part of this enterprise. She did not belong here any more.

She looked around. Nobody seemed to be aware of her or curious about her presence. But then Jenn waved her card. Jim Russett turned his head towards it and clearly caught sight of Jill. She could see him falter.

'Fifty pounds!' Jenn called out.

There was a tiny silence then Jim caught himself and he said in a slightly overloud voice, 'Fifty pounds to start. Do I have £55?'

The bidding continued smoothly and Jenn triumphantly held up her card at the end, having secured the Moorcroft vase she had admired.

'Why did you do that?' Jill whispered. 'He's seen me now.'

'I wanted that vase,' Jenn said. 'And it seemed a good idea to get him started thinking.'

'I don't know. I thought maybe we'd surprise him afterwards.'

It was clear, as the sale drew to a close, that Jim Russett was very aware of Jill's presence, stealing glances in her direction every now and again.

'Come on,' Jenn said and pulled Jill from the sofa while the rest of the buyers turned the page for the last few items in the sale.

'What are you doing?' Jill protested.

'We're going to lurk somewhere he can't get away from us. With two of us, we'll stop him getting away, then you can grill him.'

'I don't want to grill him…'

But at that moment Jim Russett appeared from the sale room. Jenneva stepped out neatly in his way and he was forced to stop immediately in front of Jill.

'Jill,' he said. 'I saw you in the sale…'

'Hello, Jim,' she said. 'I wonder, could we have a word – in private…?'

He looked around him, obviously uncomfortable. The corridor was beginning to fill with buyers leaving the saleroom.

'Well, it isn't very convenient…'

'Please, Jim. You were Hugo's friend. So humour me, just this once. Please. I won't keep you long. There's something you need to know – and I need to know…'

'You'd better come along to my office,' he said.

'I'll wait for you,' Jenn told her. 'Anyway I've got to pay for that lovely vase.'

In Jim's office, he set down his papers, offered Jill a seat, and then sat down heavily behind his desk.

'I really can't think what we've got to talk about,' he started in a dull voice but Jill interrupted him.

'I do. I'm sure you couldn't believe it when Hugo died and all this stuff came out about his affair with that woman, the flat in Bath, embezzlement from the firm…'

'I trusted him absolutely… You're right. I couldn't believe it but there it was in black and white.' Jim sighed heavily, deep furrows of sadness etched into his face.

'Didn't it occur to you to wonder why he'd embezzle such a small amount that he could have easily managed on a credit card? We weren't in any financial difficulties. And you knew I had a good job…'

'I know, but there *was* money missing…'

'Which paid for the lease of a flat in Bath – for one month only. And I can prove that he never went there. In fact, I can prove it wasn't Hugo's signature on the lease for the flat, nor the documents for setting up the bank account the embezzled money went into. It was forged – not too bad a forgery, but definitely not Hugo's signature.'

Jim rubbed his hands over his eyes. 'Hang on a minute, Jill. I don't understand…'

'Neither do I, but I'm working on it.' She continued quickly, 'Everything I've found out so far makes me think that someone set up the whole thing to discredit Hugo, to blackmail him or something…'

'But who? And why? Hugo was the straightest man on earth…'

'I know and I'm puzzled too. I think I'm getting closer to the truth but there's one tiny piece of the jigsaw that you may be able to help me with.'

'Look, Jill, the whole thing sounds far-fetched – but then Hugo's death and all that was unbelievable. You say the signatures were forged? You're sure?'

Jill nodded.

'That makes a difference, a big difference,' Jim said, taking a breath. He squared his shoulders. 'OK. Fire ahead. If I know anything that will help you, I'll be happy to tell you.'

'Thank you, Jim. I appreciate that. And if we can clear this up, then it will be good for the firm as well as clearing Hugo's reputation.' Jill paused and marshalled her thoughts. 'What I want to find out is what happened after the take-over. Was there anything different in what Hugo was doing? Did he seem any different, say anything…?'

Jim leaned back in his chair and closed his eyes as he thought hard.

'We were all working flat out over the take-over, Hugo particularly. All the financial stuff needed to be sorted out. He was up in Birmingham a lot but he had a good team down here so that wasn't a problem. It's a funny little operation up there but we thought it had potential and would give us a city outlet we could build on. We had money to invest, and they were pretty close to the ropes.'

He pulled a large diary with padded black covers from his desk drawer and flipped back over the pages.

'Let me see. We all swore we'd have a break when the take-over was through and we could take some time off but of course we never did. I've always been as much of a workaholic as Hugo, but James Wheatley, the Birmingham Finance Director, had a young family that he'd been neglecting so we persuaded him to take a couple of weeks off. Everything seemed fine. Hugo could run James's patch as well as his own. It just meant being a bit more hands-on.'

'And more time in the Birmingham office?'

'A bit more, though Hugo had had the systems networked so he could monitor everything from here.' Jim sighed again. 'Jill, I'm sorry. I really can't think of anything else.'

'Please try,' Jill pleaded. 'Did anything at all out of the ordinary happen?'

Jim riffled through his diary, his brow furrowed as he thought back.

'There was that incident with the Worcester fruit plates,' he said thoughtfully.

'What was unusual in that?' Jill asked. 'You handle a lot of Worcester.'

'We do, but we don't drop it!' Jim told her indignantly. 'That lot in Birmingham – they have a different system from ours – a sort of conveyor belt of staff moving the stuff from hand to hand once it's been sold. Well, a couple of the staff were having an argument about something and they weren't paying proper attention to what they were doing.'

Jill could only smile at the waves of disapproval emanating from Jim.

'There was a set of Worcester fruit plates – beautiful things in pristine condition. They had just come under the hammer and after some pretty brisk bidding had fetched a rather good price – £1400 if I remember rightly. Anyway, one of those clowns wasn't paying attention and fumbled the pass. Crash! Three of the six plates smashed to smithereens! The vendor was not pleased, I can tell you!'

'So what happened?'

'We had to claim on the insurance. Hugo dealt with it since James was away. It did mean extra work for him. The Birmingham office was using a different insurance company from us and we hadn't got around to harmonising that side of things.'

'And when did James come back from holiday?'

Jim consulted his diary again.

'On the Monday after the sale. I know Hugo wanted to talk to him about the accident. And I wanted to make sure the staff up there were better trained so it never happened again. I can't remember the last time such a thing happened in the Ilminster rooms. It really does a firm's reputation no good.'

An urgent knocking on the door was followed by Jenn bursting into the room.

'Sorry to interrupt,' she said with a winning smile at Jim, but the face she turned to Jill was deadly serious. 'I think we need to go. *Now*!'

'Right,' Jill said, startled by her friend's urgency. 'Jim, thank you…'

But Jenneva was pulling her arm. 'Come *on*! You've got to get out of here!'

Jill threw an apologetic smile at Jim as she allowed herself to be hurried from the room and down the corridor to the car park.

'What's the hurry? What's happened?'

But Jenn merely bundled Jill into the car and with a screech of tyres and a shower of gravel, hauled the Range Rover from its parking space and on to the road. She was silent as she concentrated on manoeuvring through the narrow village streets but once they reached the main road, she slowed a little.

'Are you going to tell me what that was all about?' Jill demanded. 'I was just beginning to get somewhere!'

'So was someone else,' Jenn said darkly. 'I spotted your friend James Wheatley and that horrid woman, his faithful secretary. He seems to be dogging your footsteps. I didn't think you'd want to bump into him.'

CHAPTER 28

✤

'I KNOW YOU'LL hate me for saying this, but I really think you should go back to your mother's,' Jenn said seriously.

'You're right,' Jill said calmly, sipping the cappuccino Jenn had bought for her at the roadside café where she had finally stopped the mad-dash getaway in the Range Rover.

Jenn looked surprised. 'You'll go to your mother's? I must admit I didn't expect you to…'

'No way. I just agree that I hate you for saying it.'

They looked at each other for a moment then began to laugh. Fairly weak laughter, but laughter.

'You're crazy,' Jenn said affectionately.

'I'm not so sure about that,' Jill said. 'I think I may be the sanest person involved in all of this. In fact, I'm sure now I have a pretty good idea of what happened and how. And I can understand why the person behind it is panicking.'

'Tell,' Jenn said simply, and planted her elbows firmly on the table. 'I'm listening.'

Jill sipped her cappuccino and began: 'I think James had some kind of scam going on related to insurance.'

And she explained how all the items put into a sale had to be insured in case of accidental damage, and how there had been an accident with substantial damage to a very expensive set of Worcester fruit plates, while James was away on holiday with his family after the take-over.

'Hugo had to sort it out and that's when I reckon he discovered that something fishy was going on. Being Hugo he would have confronted James when James came back from holiday. Then instead of 'fessing up – I don't suppose he could if his job was at risk, and there's his wife and the daughters who adore him to consider. How could he live with that? – James set up this convoluted scheme to discredit Hugo and blackmail him. I suppose James thought he could buy Hugo's silence.'

'But he didn't know Hugo,' Jenn interposed.

'Right. Hugo wouldn't have bowed to anything like that – and anyway, he would have assumed nobody would have believed a word of it.' A gurgle of laughter escaped Jill. 'Oh, poor Hugo! He was always so upstanding and respectable – yet we were all fooled for a while…' The humour faded from her face and she sighed. 'Even me.' Her eyes filled with sadness.

Jenn cut in briskly. 'So James embezzled enough to cover the deposit and the first month's rent, opened the account, set up the lease of the flat…'

Jill shook herself out of the sudden attack of the miseries and focused again. 'That's right. And I think somehow he got into our house. We had a funny break-in but it didn't look like anything had been taken so we didn't go to the police.'

'I remember you telling me about it and thinking at the time it was a bit weird.'

'I reckon James took Hugo's favourite shirt, a couple of pairs of cufflinks including one pair that was waiting to go to be repaired, and a few other things to make the photograph of the flat look more credible – things we wouldn't have missed.'

'That's nasty,' Jenn observed. 'It sounds rather cold and premeditated. It would take a lot of planning.'

'Well, finance folk are a bit like that – cold, detached, good at planning…'

'Not a bundle of fun,' Jenn said, then remembering that Hugo came into that category too, choked on a mouthful of coffee and croaked, 'Sorry, Jill. I didn't mean…'

'Well, maybe I did mean Hugo too. He was very like that – which is why I didn't notice anything was worrying him. He just didn't let it show.'

'So what do you think happened then?' Jenn asked.

'I'm not sure. I think when it became obvious that Hugo wasn't going to play ball, James decided he had to be got rid of. The blackmail scheme would suggest a motive for suicide – Hugo being so ashamed of being found out…'

'It was an overdose, wasn't it?'

'Co-proxamol, yes. Hugo had been having a lot of pain with his arthritis a few months before and there was a locum doctor who prescribed a rather large amount to tide him over. Hugo kept them in his bedside table, along with the cufflinks, the clock, his indigestion pills, that sort of thing.'

'So you think James nicked them?'

'Yes. And somehow got them into Hugo – but I can't work out how.'

'How much of this can you take to the police?' Jenn asked. 'A lot of it is just piecing together clues, snippets of coincidences, vague ideas…'

'I know. Geoffrey said he'd talk to a friend of his in the police force but I really don't feel I've got anything concrete to tell them. Though the cufflinks are interesting evidence. Trying to sell them was a bad mistake.'

'I don't think trying to shove you under a train was particularly clever either.'

'Well, at least it didn't work. And it tells me that James knows I'm on to him.'

'You've got to be very careful, Jill,' Jenneva said. 'I wish I could be around more but what with the farm and my painting, and – I have to admit – I'm spending quite a bit of time on a rather fun extra-mural interest at the moment…'

Jill raised her eyebrows.

'The current man,' Jenn explained briefly. 'Bit on the side. You know.'

'No, I don't!' Jill said.

'Well, maybe it's time you did,' Jenn told her robustly. 'You're footloose and fancy free, no ties. The world's your oyster – and there's lots of lovely men out there who'll be only too happy to stop you feeling lonely.'

'I don't think I'm ready for that, yet,' Jill said. 'In fact, I can't imagine ever being ready. When I married Hugo, I thought, good, all that silly nonsense is over now. I don't have to worry about men and having boyfriends and…'

'I can't believe it!' Jenn said. 'That's the most fun there is. It's what keeps me alive!' And she did look vibrant and happy.

'He must be rather special,' Jill said wonderingly.

'Well, he's more fun than Frank – though that's not saying much!'

'I think it's you who's crazy!' Jill stated.

'Ah, back where we started,' Jenn said triumphantly. 'Now then, are you going to your mother's or not?'

'Not,' Jill said decisively.

'So what are you going to do? Go to the police?'

'I really don't have enough of what they would consider evidence,' Jill said. 'I think they'd be kind and pat me on the head and send me on my way.' She shook her head. 'No, I don't think that would help.'

'So?'

'So I'm going to go home and potter around the house until I have a better idea. I think I want to work through Hugo's computer again and see if there's anything there that James might have missed. I'll keep the chain on the front door and I'll ring my friends each day so they know I'm all right, and I'll just let the little grey cells get to work.'

'And if James turns up?'

Jill was startled. 'I wouldn't think he'd have the nerve, do you?'

'He might, especially if he's panicking. He might want to find out exactly how much you know, what you've guessed…'

'Well, I'll cross that bridge if and when I come to it,' Jill said decisively and drained her cappuccino. 'Now, shall we have another or are you going to drive me home – at a slightly more sedate pace this time?'

CHAPTER 29

❈

Jenn was still fussing when she dropped Jill off at her house.

'I'm sorry I'm not going to be around. I've told Frank that I'm going to my mother's for the weekend but it should be a lot more fun than that!' She laughed, her face coming alive and her eyes sparkling.

'The new man?' Jill enquired.

'Well, he's not that new. Been around about three months and it's still good!' Jenn's smile was Cheshire Cat broad. 'We're off for a dirty weekend – somewhere he knows in the Cotswolds. So you just be careful while I'm away. I'll catch up with you when I come back.'

She planted a kiss on Jill's cheek then hurried back to the Range Rover. A wave and the vehicle was off in a rattle of gravel.

Jill was pondering Jenn's enthusiastic adultery when the phone rang. Jill hesitated. Who knew she was here? Was it safe to answer? She waited while the Answermachine clicked in and she could hear the voice at the other end. Quickly she picked up the phone.

'Monica! It's good to hear your voice,' she said.

'And yours,' Monica told her. 'Geoffrey told me you were home and what happened at Birmingham New Street Station. We saw it in the papers and I told Geoffrey it was as likely for you to commit suicide as Hugo.' Monica's voice brooked no disagreement and Jill was warmed by her loyalty.

'Well, you're right on both counts,' she said 'and now I'm sure Hugo didn't commit suicide. In fact, I think I've just about worked it all out.'

'Good for you!' Monica said. 'Look, I'm at the school doing a bit of admin sorting out. Can I come round when I've finished, about six, and catch up with you then? You can tell me what you've worked out, then we can present it all to Geoffrey and he'll jolly well have to listen! He's got good contacts with the police. They'll be able to pick it up and take it from there.'

'I'd love to see you,' Jill said. 'I'm not sure that what I've got really holds water as evidence, though.'

'I'll see you at six and you can try it out on me – and a large G&T, please! I'm doing computer stuff, sorting out the records for the last few months. You know computers aren't my favourite things!'

Jill laughed. 'Well, we both went into teaching because it was the teaching and being with the children that we enjoyed. See what being clever and getting promoted does for you!'

'Beast!' Monica said affectionately. 'Ah well, I'd better get on with it. I've got a couple of boxes full of computer disks in front of me that I need to work through and sort out.'

'I'll see you later, then,' Jill said. 'And I'll have that G&T ready!'

As Jill put a match to the log fire in the sitting room, Monica's mention of computers reminded her that she had planned to work through Hugo's computer again. And as she switched it on, she was reminded of James Wheatley coming to the house in the week after Hugo's death. He had told her that Hugo had been embezzling from the company but in fact, only one small sum was missing, just enough to pay for the deposit and one month's rent on the Bath flat.

James had explained that he had persuaded Jim Russett that it should be dealt with within the company, and he had asked Jill to let him check Hugo's computer. He had told her it would be better if he dealt with the matter rather than get the police involved. At the time Jill had thought James was being kind, but now she wondered had he deleted anything that might incriminate him?

While the computer warmed up, she made herself a mug of coffee and brought it back through to the study, sipping thoughtfully as she considered what she might be looking for.

Methodically, she worked her way through each of the folders and files on Hugo's computer, the email correspondence, and even Hugo's address book, but there was nothing connected to his work. Everything was social or to do with Hugo's various committees.

Finally she had to admit defeat. There was no trace of anything to do with the company.

As she rose from the table, she realised darkness had fallen so she drew the study curtains, then wandered round the house switching on lights and drawing curtains everywhere. It felt cosy and safe. She could hear the roar of the central heating boiler working away and was glad that they had not got round to replacing it with something more modern. Although the boiler was elderly, noisy, and inconveniently placed in the airing cupboard in the bathroom upstairs, it was totally reliable and Jill always felt welcomed walking into the house and hearing its roar.

The house was delightfully warm and comforting and Jill felt relaxed as she ambled into the kitchen to make a light supper for herself to eat in front of the tv. As she raked through the larder and checked the contents of the freezer, she could hear home-going cars passing by on the road outside and the occasional neighbour's car going up the lane or pulling into a nearby drive.

The crash of the cat flap in the back door startled her as Barney came hurtling in. Something must have disturbed him so Jill picked him up and petted him till he began to purr, then she set him down carefully on the floor and refilled his dish. It did not take him long to scoff the lot before he disappeared upstairs. His current most favourite snoozing place was in the airing cupboard. He had cunningly discovered how to open the door and snuggle on top of the pile of towels on the first shelf above the boiler. Jill had carefully added an old towel to the pile just for him.

Clever cats always find the warmest, cosiest place in a house, Jill thought with a smile as she turned back to the larder where she had been pondering what to have for an early supper before Monica arrived. Maybe something pasta-ish. There were a couple of cans of chopped tomatoes and a can of tuna in brine. Some leftover cheese she had spotted in the fridge would top it off before it went in the oven.

She would have to get herself sorted out and back into some kind of routine, Jill scolded herself. The larder was virtually bare. This would not do.

She was pottering round the kitchen putting the kettle on to boil for the pasta when she heard the ring of the doorbell. She looked at her watch. It was only quarter past five – too early for Monica, unless she had got finished early. Yes, that would be it. Despite her protestations that she disliked computers, Monica was actually excellent with technology and always up to the minute with the latest thing.

Jill hurried into the hallway, unhooked the security chain and pulled the front door open with a welcoming smile.

'You're early…' She stopped.

Standing on the step was not her friend Monica but James Wheatley.

CHAPTER 30

✤

'Well, you're a surprise,' Jill found herself saying as she stared at James.

'Will you let me come in? Please?' he asked. Jill was surprised at how supplicant he sounded. Taken aback, she found herself nodding and moving back into the hall so he could enter.

'I need to talk to you,' he said, and now Jill could see desperation and panic in his face. All trace of the smooth confident man had gone.

'Let's go into the sitting room,' Jill said, and was amazed at how calm and conventional she sounded, as though this were a normal visitor instead of the man she was sure had murdered her husband and had tried to kill her. She sent a fervent prayer for help and protection winging its way heavenwards, then she followed James into the sitting room.

He perched uneasily on the edge of an armchair and waited till Jill had seated herself on the opposite chair.

'I had to come,' he told her. 'You made me think. All that God stuff. It's probably too late but it's important that you know… that you understand…'

Jill felt like a headmistress again, with a pupil who had been caught in some misdemeanour brought in front of her to own up for his misdeeds and confess everything.

'Yes,' she said, and waited.

'I don't know where to begin,' James said. 'But there are things I have to tell you. You need to know.' He paused as if to catch his breath, then he said, 'You deserve to know all about it.'

She found herself nodding and agreeing. 'Yes, I think I do. But,' she added with a trace of defiance, 'I think I know quite a lot already.'

'Yes, I should imagine so.' James grinned ruefully, a trace of the boyish charm returning for a moment. 'You know, you weren't at all what I expected Hugo's wife to be like. I expected him to have a rather quiet and retiring wife but instead you're a very determined lady who won't accept things quietly.'

'I had to do something,' Jill told him. 'I knew all this rubbish about Hugo just couldn't be true. After all, I'd lived with him for nearly thirty years. I knew what kind of person he was!'

'Yes. I think that rather got forgotten – or ignored.' James sat staring into the flames of the log fire. 'I think people who have never been in a real relationship just don't know…'

'I think perhaps you should start at the beginning,' Jill directed him before he got lost down a sidetrack.

'Where it begins…' James raised haunted eyes to her face. 'Well, it begins with me doing something very stupid, something I'm not very proud of. My wife and daughters…'

He paused, then continued in a rush, 'Jill, I'm so sorry. I lied to you about that. I'm not separated. Never have been. I have a beautiful wife and two daughters that I adore.' His voice choked for a moment and he passed his hands over his eyes. 'Oh, I have been so stupid!'

'Yes,' Jill agreed.

James looked startled. 'Look, I'm sorry I…'

Jill held his gaze. 'You're sorry?' she prompted.

'I had to find out how much you knew. If I could get you to confide in me…' He looked away, embarrassed.

Jill pushed her emotions well down. 'Go on,' she encouraged him quietly.

'I was so glad to get the new job at Aston Antique Sales. I'd been made redundant from my previous job and money was getting tight, so when I got the new one it was a godsend. I felt sure it was the start of a better career for me and a better future for my family. I didn't know anything about antiques but I was fascinated from the start. It's a complicated business from the finance side, quite a challenge, but I was up for it!' His face lit with happy memories. 'In fact, I think I could have been quite good at it…' His voice trailed away.

'So what went wrong?' Jill prompted gently.

'My secretary retired and the company hired a temp…'

'Sylvia Schafer?'

'Yes. Well, you've seen her…'

'Only in the newspapers, and at the inquest.'

'Well, she's not a professional secretary. She's an actress. She was only temping while she was between parts. But she certainly knows how to act! It sounds pathetic, but I was taken in – completely bowled over, I think you could say. She was bold and glamorous, and very generous with her favours. I'd never known a woman like that. I… I had an affair with her.'

That explained the warm intimate tone on the Answermachine and James's panic that Jill had heard it. He obviously would not have wanted the affair to become public knowledge.

'And your wife?' Jill asked.

'She never knew – I took enormous care – but that annoyed Sylvia. She began to demand expensive presents so she wouldn't tell my wife.'

'Blackmail,' Jill murmured.

'Blackmail,' James agreed. 'And I didn't have enough money to buy her silence. We had a big new mortgage, school fees for the girls…'

'So?'

James gulped and seemed to shrink. He stared down at the carpet rather than meet her eyes as he continued to talk. 'She came up with a scheme for creaming money off the company. It was clever, I give her credit for that.'

'Insurance?' Jill asked quietly.

James looked startled. 'You knew? How did you find out?'

'I only worked it out today,' Jill told him. 'I had a chat with Jim Russett after the sale this morning and he mentioned the accident with the Worcester fruit plates and how Hugo had to deal with the insurance claim because you were on holiday.'

'That's right,' James admitted. He added almost defiantly, 'I'm sure we'd never have been found out otherwise. But I needed that holiday. I was desperate to spend time with my wife and family, to rebuild what I'd so nearly thrown away. I had told Sylvia that the affair was over. I thought I could straighten everything out, put it all right…'

'But that was when Hugo found out you were stealing money from the firm?'

James winced at her words. Just then the phone in the hall rang. James looked up hopefully at the interruption.

'No,' Jill said. 'I'll pick up the message later. This is much more important. Go on.'

'OK,' James said slowly. 'What happened was that Hugo discovered that the insurance company the firm was paying money to wasn't an insurance company at all. It was simply a bank account that I could pay Sylvia out of.'

'What did Hugo do?' Jill asked.

'He was brilliant,' James said. 'He took me out of the office for a bite of lunch and then simply laid out before me what he had discovered. He told me that so long as I sorted it all out – and he gave me a very reasonable deadline – no legal action would be taken. And he said it would be better for me to look for another job.'

'But you didn't take his advice?'

'How could I? The minute I got back to the office, Sylvia was on my back. "He knows, doesn't he?" she was screaming at me and I had to admit that he did. "Don't think I'm going to let you just walk away," she was yelling. "But what can we do?" I asked her. I couldn't think. I was distraught, I suppose. My whole life was crumbling in front of me. "Don't you worry," she said, smiling that cat smile of hers. "I think we can contain him." I'd no idea what she was thinking of but I was willing to go along with anything that would save my job, my family, my life…'

Again the voice faded and there was silence as James stared intently at the carpet. The phone rang again, then cut off abruptly as though the caller had lost patience.

Jill ignored the phone. She swallowed her rising fury and disgust at James's revelations as she tried to get him talking again.

'And Mrs Schafer's plan was another spot of blackmail? She set up the flat in Bath, didn't she?'

'It was her idea,' James acknowledged.

'And which of you two broke in here to get the bits and pieces to make the photograph convincing?' Jill asked icily.

James looked startled.

'I worked it out, especially when I found Hugo's cufflinks for sale at the auction the other day,' Jill explained. 'Are you going to admit it?'

'It wasn't me,' James protested. 'She broke in. I didn't know anything about it till later. But I admit that I was involved in setting up the lease…'

'Embezzling the deposit and the first month's rent payment, making it look like it was all Hugo's doing, forging his signature to get the driving licence, and on the bank documents and the lease…?' Implacably Jill listed everything she had found out.

Again, James seemed startled. 'You *have* worked it all out,' he said, almost with admiration. 'Yes, that was me. It was so simple. I thought it would surely work without causing any real harm.'

Jill snorted at James's wilful ingenuousness and concentrated on the sequence of events.

'Then what?' she demanded.

James sighed. 'Hugo's deadline arrived and he came to the Birmingham office to check that I had sorted everything out. Instead, we had taken that photograph of the flat. I showed him the picture and told him that if he didn't play ball, we'd spread all about the embezzlement and his affair with Sylvia Schafer to the newspapers.'

'How did he react?' Jill was curious to know.

'He looked at me in blank amazement, and then he began to laugh.'

'He *laughed*?' Jill echoed.

James seemed to be playing the scene back in his head as he replied, 'He said his wife would never believe he'd get involved with a "raddled old bag" like Sylvia. In fact he said he "reckoned his next-door neighbour's mangy old mongrel held more attraction for him than her". He just shook his head and kept on laughing. No, he said, nobody who knew him in the slightest would believe a word of it.'

There was silence while Jill digested this. Hugo's comment about Sylvia Schafer had warmed her heart. The reassurance that Hugo had truly preferred his own wife to the artifice of the actress cum secretary Sylvia Schafer was a welcome boost. And Jill needed it to steel her resolve for the question she now had to ask.

'So that's why you had to kill him? Because the blackmail didn't work?'

James's head came up sharply at that.

'Kill him? You didn't think…? No, I didn't kill him!'

CHAPTER 31

✦

'DON'T THINK YOU can deceive me, James Wheatley! There's no way that Hugo would have killed himself. He had no reason to do such a thing. You said yourself that he laughed at your pathetic attempt at blackmail. Why then would he feel any need to take his own life?'

James held his hands up, placatingly.

'I didn't say that,' he protested. 'I didn't say Hugo killed himself…'

Silence slammed down between them. James was leaning forward, his eyes pleading with Jill to listen to him. Jill had shot bolt upright and was staring at him.

'You're not saying Hugo killed himself? You agree it wasn't suicide?' The words seemed to form themselves from Jill's shocked brain as she tried to make sense of what James was telling her.

James nodded.

'Then… if you didn't kill him, and he didn't commit suicide…?'

James launched into explanation: 'You know Hugo had been suffering from indigestion…'

'Stress,' Jill snapped. 'And I thought it was the take-over! I should have known there was more to it than that! Hugo had loads of experience. The take-over should have been straightforward for him.'

James looked old and very sad.

'Yes, I agree. However, I reckoned he was getting an ulcer or something like that. He always had those soluble indigestion pills with him…'

And suddenly Jill could see what had happened. It would have been quite easy for someone who knew Hugo well enough to be aware of the indigestion problem.

'So someone substituted the co-proxamol… or put the co-proxamol in the indigestion mixture?' she asked.

James nodded again. 'Hugo and I met, late on Friday afternoon. He'd said if I refused to sort things out, he'd have no choice but to tell Jim Russett everything and then the police would be called in. I was in total despair, and a last blasting from Sylvia Schafer before I left the office didn't help. She told me that she'd make sure I lost everything – not just my job, but my wife and daughters too. She meant it too. I went home but I didn't get any sleep, worrying about it all night. I couldn't see what I could do.' He paused, then went on, 'I knew Hugo wouldn't drive home that evening…'

'He hated Friday night commuter traffic,' Jill agreed.

'In the morning, I thought maybe Hugo would ring me before he left for home, to give me a last chance. Maybe we could work something out… But he was waiting for me to ring him. He had stayed in his hotel until early afternoon on Saturday. I only just caught him.'

'So you called him – on his mobile?'

'Yes.'

'And?' Jill prodded.

'He agreed to see me.'

'Where?'

'I suggested we meet on Brean Down. He'd told me about the fort and I'd taken the girls there once. It was on his way. I thought the least I could do was not mess up his journey home.'

'Thoughtful,' Jill commented drily. 'So what happened?'

'We met in the car park. Hugo suggested we go for a walk so we did that, up onto the top and along to the fort, thrashing it out. I tried to get him to see what a fix I was in… but he was implacable. What I'd done was wrong...'

'Good old Hugo,' Jill said, but the irony was lost on James.

'We hadn't got anywhere and Hugo decided to pack it in and go home. We had gone all the way to the fort and now turned to start walking back to our cars when Hugo had one of those nasty indigestion spasms. He reached for one of his tablets but he didn't have any water to dissolve it in. At the Birmingham office we have a supply of mineral water in those little green plastic bottles…'

Jill remembered after the inquest the group from the firm, standing outside, drinking from green plastic mineral water bottles and Jenneva commenting acidly on how she'd got her husband to smuggle in whisky and red wine for her in similar bottles when she was last in hospital. She had said the nurses could not spot anything wrong through the green plastic.

So that was how it was done. The co-proxamol must have been dissolved in the water in advance. Hugo would have dropped in the indigestion tablet, let it fizz, then knocked it back without noticing anything was the matter. The strong peppermint flavour of the indigestion mixture would have covered up anything untoward.

But James had said he had not killed Hugo, so who was the someone who had cold-bloodedly prepared the lethal mixture and offered it to Hugo? Who else was there?

'But if it wasn't you…' Jill began slowly as her mind raced ahead.

A sudden yowl from upstairs was followed by the thunder of Barney the cat tearing down the stairs and slamming out of the cat flap in the back door.

'What on earth was that about?' Jill exclaimed and rose to go and see but James put his hands on her shoulders and stopped her.

'No, Jill. Don't go. Please stay here while I go and see.' James hesitated. 'I came here to warn you – to tell you everything so you'd understand, so you'd be safe.' He swallowed hard. 'But I seem to have messed it up again.'

'What do you mean?'

'I think someone's just scared your cat and that means there's someone else in the house. Someone who shouldn't be here. My guess is that I've been followed – just as I was to the meeting with Hugo on Brean Down.'

Jill's brain was frantically piecing together the information. It pointed in only one direction.

'I'm sorry I've brought all this on you,' James said as he crossed towards the door, 'but if you'd left everything alone…'

'Instead of poking my nose in?' Jill said. 'Stirring things up?'

'You really shouldn't have come to Birmingham. Buying the cufflinks showed that you knew more than was safe.' James sighed. 'She's killed once, then she tried to push you under the train…'

'She?' Jill asked, but she had already worked out the answer. She waited only for confirmation.

'Sylvia, Sylvia Schafer,' James said. 'She was livid when Hugo wouldn't take the blackmail seriously. She heard what he said about her. She was listening in the outer office. I've never seen such pure evil on anyone's face…'

'So she killed him. She gave him the co-proxamol solution deliberately to kill him.' It was a flat statement. 'Did you wait together to make sure it worked?' Jill challenged him bitterly.

'No!' James protested.

'So you just walked away?'

'I didn't know, did I?' James said. 'I thought it was just water. Hugo told me to go on back to my car and he picked up the bottle, popped his indigestion pill in it, gave it a shake and started knocking it back.'

'So you left him to die?'

'I didn't know!' James repeated. 'I was in a state. My life was ruined. All I could think of was getting home and somehow telling my wife…'

A sudden thought occurred to Jill. 'Hugo had his mobile with him. Why didn't he phone for help when the drug started to take effect?'

'I don't know,' James said. 'I shouldn't think his mobile would work down there at the fort. I'm sorry, Jill. I really don't know.'

A noise from upstairs of a cupboard door being closed stopped their conversation.

'You think she's here?' Jill asked quietly.

James nodded and opened the sitting room door a fraction, leaning into the gap so he could listen.

'I've no idea what she thinks she's up to but it's not going to be good,' he whispered. 'Time to find out, I think.' And in a rapid move, the door was open and James was bounding up the stairs.

'Oh no, you don't,' Jill shouted after him. 'I'm not being left out. Not now.' And she followed quickly to find James flinging open all the doors on the upstairs corridor.

'What do you think you're doing?' Jill heard him yell.

'Tidying up loose ends,' came the calm response from the bathroom.

'In a bathroom?' was James's incredulous reply.

'Well, why don't you hang around and see if you can work it out,' Sylvia Schafer mocked him as she emerged, perfectly coiffed and made-up, in a smart business suit. 'Ah, Mrs Leiston, I'm going now,' she told Jill coolly as she walked towards her.

'Not bloody likely,' Jill exploded and launched herself at her.

'Don't be stupid!' Sylvia Schafer exclaimed and tried to sidestep the attack.

'That's the mistake you made,' Jill said breathlessly as she got her in a sure grip. 'Neither Hugo nor I was stupid. If anyone's stupid, it's you and I'm not letting you away with any of this!'

Sylvia Schafer tore at Jill with her nails but Jill refused to let go. The two women wrestled, each as determined as the other, grabbing handfuls of hair and clothes to gain advantage until they overbalanced and fell onto the floor in Jill's bedroom.

Jill was first to get to her feet. Her eyes darted round the room for a weapon and her eyes seized on the urn on the mantelpiece containing Hugo's ashes. She grabbed for it as Sylvia Schafer stumbled for the door.

Hanging on to the urn, Jill flung herself at her back.

'Oh no, you don't!'

Sylvia Schafer turned round, taking in quickly what Jill was holding.

'Don't be ridiculous!' she sneered. 'A cheap plastic urn is going to stop me?'

Fury surged through Jill. With one fast unthinking movement, she pulled off the lid of the urn, scooped out a handful of the ashy mix of pulverised bone splinters and fine wood ash and flung it full in Sylvia Schafer's face.

'Try that!' she gasped. 'See how close you can be to my dead husband now!'

Sylvia Schafer recoiled in horror as she clawed at her face trying to clear it of the ashes, blindly turning and crashing down the stairs.

'Don't think you'll get away!' Jill screamed after her.

'Oh, I will,' Sylvia Schafer spluttered through ashy lips as she pulled open the front door and ran into the garden.

Jill, still clutching the urn, staggered on to the path after her. A few steps towards the gate, she stopped. The lane was filled with vehicles. At least two were police cars with lights flashing, and two burly policemen had seized Sylvia Schafer very firmly between them and were leading her to one of the cars.

At that moment, a loud explosion flung Jill to the ground as her house burst into flames. As she fell, Jill remembered

James. Before she lost consciousness, she frantically shouted his name.

'James! James is in there! Somebody get James out!'

CHAPTER 32

BASICALLY, SHE JUST felt rather muzzy and bruised. As she tried to clear her thoughts, Jill remembered the explosion which had sent her flying onto the paved path in her garden. Gingerly she tried first one knee then the other, then flexed her arms. She had come down rather heavily, but it seemed apart from understandable bruises and some aches and pains, she had not come to any real harm.

It took a moment to register that she was not in her own bed. Forcing herself to open her eyes and concentrate, she realised she was in a hospital bed in a small room on her own. Probably in for observation or just making sure she was all right, Jill decided pragmatically. Well, she was.

Then she remembered James. Had they got him out in time? Was he here in this hospital? Did his wife know? She reached for a bell or a buzzer to call a nurse and in seconds a concerned girl in uniform was at her side.

'No, no, I'm fine!' Jill insisted. 'James? The man who was in my house. Is he all right?'

'I'll have to find out,' the nurse said. 'Just rest. Would you like something to drink?'

Jill looked at her suspiciously.

'No, I don't want anything to drink. I want to find out what happened…'

'I'll get someone,' the nurse stammered and hurried out.

The someone turned out to be a plain-clothes policeman, who flipped open his wallet to reveal official identification.

'Five minutes,' the nurse told him as she held open the door.

He sat down in the chair by Jill's bedside and looked closely at her.

'I'm fine,' Jill stated bluntly. 'Bruised and a bit sore, but no injuries as far as I can tell. What's more, my brain is working perfectly and I want to know what happened.'

She was surprised by the sudden grin that flashed across the policeman's face before it was replaced by a stern businesslike look.

'OK, Mrs Leiston,' he said. 'I'm Detective Inspector Peter Aldridge. What can you remember about last night?'

'You mean I have to show you mine before you show me yours?'

Jill was pleased to see the grin flash again. He was actually rather good looking. Jenneva in her place would be flirting like mad. Jill quelled the frivolous thought and told herself firmly it was hysteria, post-traumatic whatever. She made her face look calm as if she were in perfect control.

The detective was responding straightforwardly to her question. 'Something like that. We need to hear from you what you experienced before we mess up your memories with our side of it.'

'I understand.' Jill set herself to remember and report clearly. 'I was at home when James Wheatley turned up. I'd been investigating the circumstances of my husband's death. I wasn't at all satisfied that it was suicide.'

'Yes, we knew that.'

Jill darted an enquiring glance at him.

'Your friend Monica Harris has been badgering her husband to talk to me.'

'Ah, the police contact. Good for Monica,' Jill murmured. 'I've been badgering Geoffrey too.'

The grin popped up again briefly. 'So he said.'

'I'd uncovered some damning evidence which had alerted the people involved… James Wheatley and Sylvia Schafer.'

Peter Aldridge consulted his notebook.

'The Finance Director at your husband's firm and his secretary?'

'That's right. James turned up at my door late yesterday afternoon. I was expecting Monica and I opened the door without thinking. Yes, I know I should have been more careful!' Jill said to forestall any criticism. 'I thought he'd come to warn me off, threaten me, maybe even finish off the job. You know I was pushed almost underneath a train at Birmingham New Street…'

'Yes,' he said. 'We know that now.'

'Good.' Jill paused and sorted through her memory of what happened. 'Instead James seemed to want to confess everything. It was very odd. I felt like a schoolmistress listening to a naughty small boy. He was perfectly open about everything…'

'Everything?'

'Absolutely. How he'd been drawn into an affair with Sylvia Schafer who had started to blackmail him. He told me how he'd set up a scam inside the Birmingham company before the take-over, creaming off the insurance payments to pay her off. How my husband had found out and given him time to put it right… only he didn't. I don't think Sylvia Schafer would let him. She's the real villain in all of this,' Jill added fiercely.

'Keep going,' Peter Aldridge encouraged her.

'She had the idea of blackmailing Hugo. It seems to be a major trick in her repertoire. Between them, she and James set up the rental of a flat in Bath, paid for through a bank account they opened in Hugo's name with a lump of money James embezzled from the firm. She was behind a funny little break-in we had. She took a few things to make the photograph of the flat look more convincing. And then they told Hugo.'

'And?'

'He laughed at them. Well, nobody would believe such a story, nobody that knew Hugo! Anyway he rather unwisely said something uncomplimentary about Sylvia Schafer and that basically signed his death warrant.'

'How did they do it?'

'Not *they*. James was genuinely horrified at the idea that he had killed Hugo, I'm sure of that,' Jill insisted. 'It was that woman on her own. She was acting as Hugo's secretary while Penny, his own secretary, was on holiday. They knew Hugo had been taking soluble antacids for his indigestion and he had an attack the last time he and James met, down at the fort on Brean Down. James reckoned Sylvia Schafer had dissolved a lethal dose of co-proxamol in a bottle of mineral water which she then offered Hugo when he needed water to dissolve the indigestion tablet he always took. She had been keeping tabs on James and had followed him to his meeting with Hugo. Anyway, Hugo accepted the bottle of water, popped his indigestion tablet in it and drank it off.'

'Mmm, planned in advance. That's very cool,' the detective commented.

'Cold and calculating,' Jill said. There was silence as she thought of Hugo, dying there and unable to ring anyone for help...

'Hugo's mobile wasn't in the sack of things I was given. Do you think it might still be lying around up there?' A sudden thought prompted Jill to ask, 'Or did that woman take it?'

'We can ask her.'

'I suppose she would have just thrown it away,' Jill mused. 'Would you be able to find it now?'

'It's possible,' the detective said, but Jill could tell that the time that had passed made it unlikely.

'Were you aware that Sylvia Schafer was in your house?' he prompted her.

'No,' Jill said. 'I was completely absorbed in what James was saying. I'd been convinced he had been solely responsible for Hugo's death and I was determined to hear the truth.' She thought back. 'I did hear the cat rush out of the house. That's what alerted us. James insisted on going upstairs to see. That's when he found Sylvia Schafer... I'm not sure what she was doing. She was in the upstairs bathroom... James challenged her and she laughed at him and tried to just walk out of the house.' Jill paused for breath. 'The cheek of the woman!' Jill recalled angrily. 'She thought she could just walk past me...'

'So what happened?'

'I grabbed her. It was a real cat-fight!' Jill laughed shakily. 'I should be quite ashamed of myself – but I'm not. I'd have done anything to stop her! I went for her with my nails, and grabbed handfuls of her hair!'

'Where was James during this?' Peter Aldridge asked.

Jill tried to think back. 'I think he was still in the bathroom, trying to work out what Sylvia Schafer had been doing.'

'And Sylvia Schafer, she left him to it?'

'She got loose and was making rapidly for the stairs. I grabbed Hugo's ashes. I've been keeping them in an urn on my bedroom mantelpiece till I got this all sorted out and I could think what to do with them, have a proper funeral, that sort of thing.' Jill explained.

'And?'

'Well, she was trying to get away and I didn't want her to, so I scooped out a handful of the ashes and flung them in her face… to blind her and slow her down, I suppose.'

'Ah, that explains it,' Peter Aldridge murmured.

'Explains what?' Jill asked.

'She was scrubbing at her face when she stumbled out of the house as if she couldn't see where she was going. That's why she didn't see us…'

'I came charging out after her,' Jill remembered 'and I saw two policeman had grabbed her.'

'Your friend Geoffrey rang us,' Peter Aldridge explained. 'Monica had found something on one of the disks she was working on at school…'

'Oh yes, she was sorting out some admin stuff before she came over to see me.'

'That's right and she found a strange disk – not a school one – but one containing all the evidence Hugo had collected and his notes on the whole situation. She recognised immediately what it was. She tried to ring you…'

Jill remembered the phone ringing. She had decided to ignore it because she did not want to disturb James while he was in flow. The phone had rung a second time and then cut off…

'That's right. When she didn't get an answer, she rang the second time. I reckon Sylvia Schafer pulled the phone lead out of the socket. When Monica tried a third time, and you still didn't answer that worried her. She rang Geoffrey and told him everything. He rang me and I decided it was worth coming over, with a few friends just in case.'

'I'm glad. Good for Monica – and good for Hugo. He must have put the disk in the box on my desk the night of the Parents Evening when he was waiting for me in my office.' Jill sighed. 'So it's all over. You've got both James and Sylvia Schafer… By the way, what was she doing in my bathroom? Oh, wait a moment, the explosion… my house… James…?' It all came rushing out with increasing anxiety.

'Calm yourself! Please, calm down, or the nurse will come and throw me out!'

'But I want to know!' Jill insisted.

'OK. What Sylvia Schafer was doing was wedging some highly inflammable aerosol cans around the boiler in the airing cupboard in your bathroom. Barbecue accelerant, in fact. She upped the boiler setting just to make sure… The cans exploded when they hit the right temperature, the explosion ripped apart the boiler and the gas pipes, and as a result the house went up. It's a bit of a mess and you won't be able to go back there for a while.'

Jill was silent for a moment as she took it all in.

'And James?'

'James didn't make it, I'm afraid. He was in the bathroom at the moment everything exploded.'

'Oh, poor James. How horrid.' Jill swallowed hard, then remembered. 'His poor wife too… and the girls…' Jill looked at the Detective-Inspector. 'He was trying to save me, though, wasn't he? I'm sure he was.'

He looked unconvinced.

'Really!' Jill insisted. 'He said he had come to see me to tell me everything so I'd be safe. I'm sure he was trying to protect me from that woman, and in the end, he was trying to work out what she had done…'

'Well, if you're sure,' the detective said soothingly 'I think we might be able to see it like that.'

'I'm glad. He never should have got involved in any of this. He was weak rather than wicked…'

'Not what anyone could say about Sylvia Schafer. She was kicking and screaming all the way to the cells! My constables have the scars to prove it!'

Jill lay back on the pillows exhausted.

'So that's that,' she said.

On the bedside table next to her, she saw the urn with Hugo's ashes and reached out to pat it.

'Well, at least I did what I set out to do. I've proved Hugo's innocence of any wrongdoing. Now I can bury him as befits the man he was. I hope you'll come to the party, Detective-Inspector?'

AUTHOR'S NOTE

❖

EAGLE-EYED READERS and those who know Somerset well will realise I have taken some liberties with locations. Although the story is set in Somerton, a town I know well, I have moved a few things around there and in other places for the sake of the story. It is fiction after all!

As always, I have a lot of people to thank for their help in bringing this book to publication. First of all, Andrew and Reggie, without whom… Then Jane, Brenda, and my friends in the Mid-Somerset Group of the United Reformed Church for their amazing support. And lastly Liz Carter of Capstone Publishing Services for her wonderful cover design and help formatting the typescript.

The research for the book was huge fun and I was surprised and delighted by how generous and helpful people were. Special mention goes to Elizabeth Talbot and Paul Head of T. W. Gaze, auctioneers in Diss; Michael Rose, West Somerset Coroner now retired; and Barbara Bourne of Birmingham Museum and Art Gallery. Last but not least my friends, Jean in Wick and Thelma in Somerset, for unstinting encouragement. Thank you!

Printed in Great Britain
by Amazon